Elemental Prey

by

Tara J. Schwenker

Mornings and nature always seem to be in perfect harmony, when in Yosemite they are a symphony. Yosemite is the one place on the western seaboard that remains untouched, pristine. It is awe inspiring yet comforting to know when we look out we see the same scenic views our ancestors and the Native Americans before them took in. Millions of years ago the Sierra Nevada was uplifted and then sloped to form the gentle western inclines and the more dramatic eastern angles. These gentle gullies and ravines are the arms these mountains cradle us with and are just as sure to rip us apart with their jagged edges and wild things unseen.

"Jilly, Jilly, Ji-ll-ly. Come here, come, come, come! Come quick, hurry!" Joey called to his sister, so excited he was almost breathless.

Jilly was busy concentrating on a butterfly cocoon she discovered hanging off of a fallen branch of a great sequoia.

"Jil-ly! Hurry up! Come on-n!" His voice carried a stern undertone for a young boy he was such an old soul.

This sounded important. She straightened up and headed toward her brothers voice, careful not to lose her footing on the moss clinging to the boulders and damp leaves leading to the water's edge.

Jilly and Joey, the two are bookends. With less than two years between them, they do everything together. Joey is smart. Some would say he's a genius. Merl and Michael don't want his intelligence to lead to elitism that they have seen happen with so many talented young minds so they always remind him how much more there is to know. "Joey, you don't know what you don't know" is one of their favorite quotes. Humility will keep him hungry as Michael always says.

Although never stoic, Joey is profound and philosophical. He has an amazing ability to piece things together, a born cryptologist. Jilly resides the other end of the spectrum. She is an artist. She feels deeper than most. She has this way of identifying with all living creatures. Empathy and compassion are her driving factors. She hears music and automatically connects to it on a different level. Jilly is as vibrant a ray of sunshine through a prism.

They are Yin and Yang, the Alpha and Omega. They are each a missing half to a whole. Even as toddlers there was never the normal competition generally seen between siblings. They had a connection from the minute they set eyes on each other. Joey would stand at the bassinette and stare at her for hours. As time went on Jilly would cry when Joey went to his room to bed. Eventually the two shared a room until Joey was five. The monitor was a lifeline between the two.

Usually only seen in twins, they seemed to have a psychic bond. Noticeable especially once they started school. One incident that stands out was when Joey fell on the playground during recess. He twisted his wrist and was whisked away to the school nurse. At that very moment

Jilly screamed out, dropped her crayon and started crying that she hurt while holding her wrist. She was in preschool, a different building more than a mile away from her brother. That episode started what would become an anomaly not only apparent but cherished between the two.

"JILLY?!?" screamed Joey, still staring down at the riverbed, entranced in his discovery. "Pssst" Jilly whispered about an inch behind from her brother. She was stealth as the Bobcats or Grey Fox that called Yosemite home. Startled, Joey lost his footing and went down with a splash, still calm and cool as a cucumber. He stood up, twisted the water from the edge of his shirt, realigned his eyeglasses and went back to his original position. Pointing he couldn't contain himself to share his discovery. "Jilly, Can you believe this? This is the best!"

2.

Back at the cabin Michael and Merleigh were cleaning up breakfast dishes and getting ready for the hike they had planned with the kids at dinner last night. Armed with maps, downloaded to their tablets and smart phones were the suggested trails. The kids made a presentation worthy or better than most of the presentation decks made at his technology firm back in the valley. The almost nine mile or so Panorama Trail awaited the Mitchell clan.

Waterfalls with secluded swimming holes, picnic areas and great photo ops, everything a vacation is supposed to be. Creating memories, the strengthening of family bonds, that's what this vacation is for. Michael had some trepidation which he chalked it up to the fact that he was almost forty and hadn't really done any type of exercise outside of the obligatory half hour at his firm's gym every few days in years.

This was the first family vacation they had enjoyed in, well, no one could really remember the last time they had spent more than a long weekend together. Merleigh was in her glory.

This is what she always wanted, what she always dreamt of since attending Texas A&M. The university is home to fifty thousand students and Merl knew when she was accepted it was also the home to her future husband. Male to female ratio, that was the primary factor in her choice of schools. Merleigh was a very smart woman whose Texan background meant that you set your goals on a handsome man who would be a good husband, and a better provider and father. Yes, as old school as that was, she knew from generations of women past that this recipe had been a blue ribbon winner and she was not going to be the one to change it.

She remembered the first time she set eyes on Michael at a mixer, a stop light party. Dressed in green, red plastic beer cup in hand she knew he was the one. She worked hard to catch him yet made Michael think he was the one to pursue her. It was an art form, and she was the master. She was a few years his junior in school, so when he graduated and took a job back home as mechanical engineer in the Bay Area she dropped her scholastic pursuits and followed hot on his trail. This too was something she always had in her bag of tricks to hoard over him when he got out of line. Poor Merl, yanked out of school in the prime of her life to sacrifice her goals and support his. She laughed when she thought of this, finding Michael or a reasonable facsimile of him was her primary intent in the first place, and she always got what she wanted.

"Dozer, you wait outside you lazy ball of fur." Dozer is an English Mastiff, a lovable one hundred and ninety seven pound lap dog. He is the family teddy bear. Jilly and he are the same age on around or about, give or take a few weeks. The Mitchell's rescued him when he was only four months old. Yes, only four months and already the size of an elementary school child the day they went to the pound to get him.

That day started out with Merl thinking about maybe getting a Chihuahua, or at the most a Golden, but never in a million years did she think she would end up with Dozer. Michael was away on business and she thought this would be a good experience for the kids to have a dog growing up. She always had one or more as a girl, and she was having a hard time without one in the house especially since Michael was away on business so much.

At the shelter they saw quite a scene, it was so emotional. The Mitchell's weren't even out of the parking lot as the spotted one of the volunteers trying to walk Dozer. The knucklehead had sat down in the middle of the street. He decided he was done for the day. At fifty five pounds at only four months, the little girl who was maybe eighty pounds soak and wet herself was having a time with him. Merl, with Jilly on her back and Joey just barely able to walk on his own went over and approached the silly scene playing out in front of them. Joey and Dozers eyes met and he lumbered straight over to us, love at first sight. Dozer was a fawn with a black mask, droopy jowls full of puppy wrinkles and huge paws. Needless to say, they never made it inside to look at another dog. He had them at woof. After filling out the paperwork and visiting the gift shop for toys, beds, bowls, a leash, and anything else doggie related, away we went the newest family member. He put his head on Joey and snored all the way home, hence the name Dozer. To this day, we can't really make him go more than fifteen or twenty yards at a time without a half hour rest period.

"Hey babe, do me a favor?" Those words always made Michael get a shiver down his spine. There, waiting at the end of that sentence was a Honey-Do list, the sweeter the tone, the worse the chore. "Start getting the stuff together for the hike. We need sunscreen, our portable phone charger- the list is on the table." Michael exhaled, although not what he wanted to be doing, this was much less severe than anticipated.

Merleigh was organized. She wanted everything perfect, her home, her clothes, her hair, her family. She went beyond organized. She was meticulous. Some would even say she was compulsive. She has the discipline of a US Marine. Yet, with all of these quirks she was gentle, loving and passionate about her family.

Michael returned to the kitchen, backpacks filled and a Cheshire grin on his face. She looked at him, somewhat suspicious, somewhat playful. What could he have up his sleeve? He has only been gone for a few minutes.

The curtains rippled in the cool morning breeze rhythmic and soothing. Something about the crisp air and the sound of the kids laughing made her feel energized in total harmony with the universe. Life is good.

3.

Michael reached around grabbing her by the waist. She struggled to break free as he pulled her backward into him. He used the back of his hand to brush the hair up off of the back of her neck. He gently exhaled, so close to her skin he made every hair on her body stand on end with electricity. She inhaled with anticipation as he gently caressed her with his lids and his tongue. She arched her back and leaned into him, feeling him harden as she moved. With a stealth hand he reached around, untying her drawstring waist, her sweats puddling around her ankles leaving her naked from the waist down. His hands were cool to the touch, moving up the concave of her belly just ever so gently sweeping her skin with his fingertips. She reached up behind her with both arms grabbing him around the neck. She stood there helpless, aching for him as he fondled her erect nipples. She moaned, ever so slightly as she gyrated her hips against him, feeling him throbbing into the small of her back. As she moved, he spread her legs stopping her with his knee. He worked his hands down her trembling body from her hardened nipples to the moist spot between her legs, gently gliding his fingers back and forth methodically sliding in and out, using his thumb to pleasure her as he did so.

He knew her body like his own. He knew she could not hold out no matter how she tried. He felt himself coming close to the brink as she started to pant, arching her back and spreading her legs even wider. He dropped to his knees, now using his mouth to caress her sacred spot while his fingers dove in and out of her, faster, faster, hotter and wetter she writhed while attempting to hold back. She shook, inhaled a sharp breath, she grabbed him and pushed his face into her until she could no longer take the teasing tip of his tongue probing at her.

Michael stood as she turned around to unzip his jeans. She bent over the counter her legs seemed to stretch on for miles. In one daft movement he was inside her, she fondled his balls in her hands, hearing him moan made her want to let go, but she let wave after wave crash through her. Harder and deeper he was a machine only concerned about his body and himself now, using her up. Grabbing the back of her hair as they both reached the final throws, she felt the earth quake inside of her, filling her with lava, a liquid fire as he pushed into her so deep he lifted her off of her feet.

A sweet sheen of sweat was all that was between them as he gently slid out of her and kissed her forehead. "Good morning sunshine."

Dang, I sure hope the kids didn't hear us out there she thought. Merl was very pleased with herself as she zipped her baby pink hoodie, though sore from the wear. Looking through the blinds, she noticed that the trees were unusually still. She bent down, pulled up her sweats, slipped on her Sketchers and adjusted the waistband so her drawstring lay just below the jutting line of her hip bones.

4.

Michael had gone in the other room to freshen up. She heard the water run in the bathroom, but she didn't hear the kids. Something wasn't right, but she wasn't going to get herself all tied up. They probably went after one furry or feathered thing. As long as they were together, they were fine.

Michael ran some cool water in the sink and splashing his flushed face. Looking himself in the mirror, he had a half grin and a twinkle in his eye of one very content man. He opened the window next to the sink for some fresh air. The cabin had one of the old crank casement windows from the fifties in there. It reminded him of the windows in his grandparents' home up north on the coast. He remembered how excited he would get when he would start to see signs for Oregon. Little memories were t00he ones that meant the most to him. Hopefully that is something he passed onto Jilly and Joey.

Speaking of Mutt and Jeff, they seemed peculiarly quiet. Whenever the two were together, you could hear incessant giggling, prodding, teasing, yelping, or squealing of one or the other. Michael held his breath and leaned over pushing his ear to the screen. Nothing, no birds, no rustling leaves, not even Merl in the kitchen. Something was wrong, very wrong.

His stomach tightened and his pulse began to race. Instantly he knew in his bones that this was the second his life was about to twist into a knot of no return. He ran down the hall bumping into Merl.

"Have you see Joey or Jilly?" Both he and Merl blurted out at the same time. Michael grabbed her arm dragging her behind him. Her eyes widened with fear as they ran out to find their children. They burst out-side with the speed and efficiency of an Olympic relay team. The screen door bouncing and slamming against the wooden frame behind them- open shut, open shut, open shut the rickety latch of the door never catching but coming to rest in itself. Its mocking echo reverberated through the silence of the canyon.

"Joey! Jilly! Come on you two. We're leaving without you if you don't come back here right now!" The word now caught in her throat, an octave above her normal tone. She tried to sound lithe and playful, but the mounting terror of something gone horribly wrong was boiling in her chest. She felt like she was hallucinating- somehow time was speeding up and standing still all at once. Her lungs tightened her rib cage compressed squeezing the last ounce of air from her torso, her throat dried and her pulse raced. Even though she was standing outside she was feeling claustrophobic, as if she was suffocating. Her body temperature rising, sweat forming on her upper lip and in the small of her chest. She couldn't catch her breath, her lungs were closing. She closed her eyes the world spinning around her. She was losing her balance. Her legs were getting weak under the weight of her own body.

"Get a grip! You are never going to make it until they are eighteen if you keep acting the fool!" The internal pep talk she had giver herself hundreds of times echoed hollow as an empty tin can.

Michael was leading in a full tear down the slight mossy incline to the edge of the water where he had last seen them playing in the morning sunlight. Using his most emphatic, firm tone he could muster, he screamed only the way a father can. "Joseph Eric Mitchell, I am telling you right now to come out from wherever you are hiding. I am not joking young man! Jillian Cassandra, this means you to! This is not a game!" Usually the middle name game put the fear of God into them and halted whatever activity they were partaking at the time. If used more than once, the siblings knew that the crime was never worth the punishment. Boredom and banishment from the family goings on were fates far worse than either could tolerate.

He stopped and turned a full three hundred and sixty degrees, surveying the woods behind them. Today, for all intents and purposes, was a perfect day. The water was quietly babbling front of them, the smell of the moisture hung in the morning air as the dew drops dried off of the leaves. The surroundings were pristine. There was nothing out of place, no sign of a struggle, not the smallest hint of an injury or trouble of any kind. Looking for a telltale sign of their kids, it seemed they had vanished without a trace from this very spot. The earth had swallowed them leaving nothing but the lingering memory of their laughter to follow.

The wilderness stretching out for miles and miles, they could be anywhere. "Merl, you go back to the cabin call for help. We need a search party. I am going to walk up and down the river. If they followed something they may be lost or hurt."

Merl just stood there, looking at Michael but looking through him. Motionless, emotionless, as if she turned back to look at Sodom and Gomorrah and was now just a pillar of salt.

"Merl, God damn it, I mean now!" Michael snapped, time was of the essence, and if push came to shove his children came first, above even their mother, his wife.

Merleigh robotically returned to the cabin. She picked up her satellite phone and dialed nine-one-one. The call went to the local dispatcher. "9-1-1 what is your emergency?"

"My children are missing:"

"Ma'am, did you say your children are missing?"

Merleigh's voice came out like a steel knife from a glacier, cold and cutting making her tongue feel like it was bleeding as she spoke. "Listen to me, carefully, my children are missing. Get someone out here right now. Do you understand me? My children are not here, and I need a search and rescue- now!" Words slicing the air, saying them made it a reality. Her children were missing.

"Ma'am, I have someone on the way. Please stay on the line so I can collect some information." The dispatcher was calm asking all of the right questions. How many children were missing? What are their names? What are they wearing? What are their ages? When were they last seen? What were they doing? What time did she last see them? Have they run off before? Was this natural for them to explore out of their comfort zones? Had there been any problems in the home? The list felt endless and repetitive. She knew why they were asking, but damn it, she needed to DO something besides parrot information. Merl just answered them numbly.

"If you are asking me is it possible that my kids ran away, you must be on fucking drugs!" Merleigh snapped. Her nerves were raw. She was on edge and nauseated by the thoughts running threw her head.

The dispatcher continued asking a myriad of questions as time crept by.

5.

Michael walked what felt like miles up and down the river. Some places the rocky shoreline disappeared and he had to walk in the water. It had been a dry season, the water never reaching above a few inches over his ankles except in random spots where fish collected themselves in cool tide pools.

Nothing his kids couldn't handle. Both had been in Scouts since they were in kindergarten, both trained for what to do in an emergency. That fact made things even worse. As he inhaled the fresh mountain air filling his lungs gave him the sensation he was breathing in needles or shards of glass. Hoping somehow his instincts would pick up the slightest essence of them and lead him directly to them he streamed on with a purpose.

On any other day the warm sun and cool clean air would recharge him. This would be one of the moments that he would file away to savor during a rough day at the office or when he was stuck in traffic, but not today.

He called out for Joey and Jilly at the top of his lungs. Deep in his heart, he knew a response would not come. If it were up to him he would forget that they had ever come to this place, turn back the hands of time and restart the past twenty four hours.

It amazed him how such a beautiful day can become so dark. He had been searching for close to an hour when he started back to the cabin. Terrible scenarios running through his mind, what if they fell down an old mine shaft, what if they go caught in a bear trap, what if they fell down a cliff into a ravine, what if a hunter… he would not allow himself to entertain a thought like that. It couldn't, it wouldn't…He had to get back. What kind of man lets something happen to his children? What kind of father was he?

Feeling apprehensive his senses went into a hyper vigilant state. As he approached the cabin he heard the tired rolling up the dust laden dirt road at the bottom of the hill. Pebbles flung out from under the speeding tires of the SUV, hitting the trees that lined the road as they made a pinging sound then a thud returning to the ground from where they originated. The Ranger's SUV slammed to a halt as two men and a German Shepherd jumped out of the vehicle.

Seeing the uniforms sent a set of shock waves through Merl. Dressed in their khaki green ranger garb and baseball caps they had a distinctive military air about them. They walked sure footed and commanded respect without having to wield their authority lie most city cops.

6.

"Mr. and Mrs. Mitchell, I'm Ranger Corpaccio and this is Ranger Sands and this here is Ranger Shep. If you don't mind, I would like to have a few words with you while Ranger Sands starts the search."

Ranger Carpaccio was the taller of the two, and despite an ethnic ring to his name he was fair of complexion, green eyed with just the right amount of freckles dotting the bridge of his nose. He was the older of the two men with crow's feet starting to form in the outer corners of his eyes, a sure sign of squinting in the sun for so many years. He had a gentle, easy smile and a warm manner that made you feel safe.

Ranger Sands displayed a boyish, charming grin which was stark contrast to dark espresso colored eyes who told of something inauspicious just below the surface. His skin was the shade of dark caramel, his hair cropped close, high and tight leaving just a hint above the collar of the tight thick curls that were once there. His arms bulged out of short sleeves that stretched over his unusually large muscles. He was stealth for a man who looked like he shouldn't be able to turn his head due to the size of the trunk of his neck.

Ranger Shep sported a thick shiny black coat covering his massive frame supported by huge paws, white teeth that stood out from the black mass of his body. If it wasn't for the vest and shine of the gold badge on his collar one could easily mistake him for a wolf without a second thought. He had the size and the gate of a wild beast.

Shep circled the two Rangers, whining and pulling to get to work. Merl bent down to pet him and Shep froze at attention, catching Merl off guard. She was not used to this type of behavior from a dog thanks in part to Dozer.

With a gentle tug of the lead Shep sat obediently staring at his partner waiting for his command. "Mam, he is on the clock and ready to work, so if you could get me something that belongs to the children? An article of clothing or a toy would suffice. Any object that will give Shep a scent to work with and preferably something they had recently."

Dozer actually stood up, raising the fur on his back and taking a protective stance eyeing the new comers, sensing something was amiss. Merl moved around the rescuers, Dozer moved closer to her, his hackles up in the air, letting out a low throaty growl from for the first time in his life. This startled both Merl and Michael for neither thought he knew how to bark, no less growl.

"Dozer, shush!" Merl grabbed his collar and led him inside as she went to retrieve the items the ranger had requested. Dozer stood his ground, leaning against her, not wanting anyone or anything out of his sight. She finally moved the massive wall of dog and corralled him into the cabin.

Once inside she went directly into the great room. Leaning down she picked up the blanket the two had fallen asleep under last night. Memories flashed of less than twelve hours prior that made her break down and cry.

Dozer leaned into her as if trying to protect her from the world. She held onto him, clutching his puppy soft fur in her hands praying for God to let her kids be alright. "Dear God, I swear, I promise I will be a better mom, a better wife, a better everything. Please let them find them. Please God, I am so sorry! Please, oh God Please!"

She was never so unsure of a prayer being heard or answered. Her faith had been strong, but today she felt that the word she spoke to an unknown entity were nothing more than a hollow attempt at changing what seemed to be destined already.

 Outside, Michael stood with the rangers. "Sir, can you tell us where the last place is you saw your children?" asked Ranger Sands. He had the SoCal yaw in his voice, probably from San Diego, navy brat or maybe LA.

Michael eyed him for a moment, surmised that he most likely graduated from some school in the not quite ghetto and found his ticket out by joining the marines then becoming a cop. Even though if he was only a ranger. Like so many law enforcement agents here. It's a way to stay out of trouble but in their neighborhoods with good pay and a secure job.

7

Sands could tell the look of mistrust in people's eyes by now. Assumptions made him see red. "Sir, for your information, I am a third generation search and rescue worker. I have lived all over the country while my father, who worked for the Federal Government, trained various agencies cutting edge tactical proficiency. I guarantee we will do our best to find Jilly and Joey."

Michael relaxed and looked ashamed, he knew better then to make assumptions, especially being half Mexican. Old habits die hard, and stress brings out the worst in people, he was guilty of that. "I am sure you will Ranger" his voice trailing off.

"Merl, hurry up!" He snapped, again. God Damn her! He needed her realize this is urgent, that time was the enemy. She had to get her ass in gear. "Merleigh!" he screamed as loud as his voice would go, though he was getting horse from yelling all morning for the kids added to the stress was making his vocal cords feel like fraying tight ropes.

Merl appeared with the fleece blanket that was their favorite. It was a queen size throw with different breeds of dogs depicted on a collage. Handing it over to the ranger she had to force herself to let it go.

"As I was saying, did either of you notice anything odd? Did you see anybody lurking around here? Did you hear anything that made you suspicious? Maybe your dog growled or barked in a certain direction? Did you see any flashes of light that may have been out of the ordinary?" Ranger Carpaccio asked in rapid fire.

"No, nothing out of the ordinary, I answered all of these questions already to the dispatcher. Please, stop standing here and help us find our children!"

Merl was getting agitated as time ticked on. She had been logical longer then her body could handle, her emotions were taking over. A mother lioness and her cubs were gone.

The sun was getting higher in the sky.

Were her babies injured? They didn't have their lunch, they must be hungry. Had they been attacked by some wild animals, did they come across venomous snakes? Her biggest fear that she would never see her children again was bubbling to the surface, and there was nothing she or anyone could do to quell those fears until her kids were home, safe and in their arms.

8.

A minute can change the course of your life, even a spilt second, a right instead of a left, crossing from one side of the street to the other, forgetting your keys. Each seemingly insignificant action can alter your future. Each event taking place in a blink of an eye, here and gone before you can process the impact. Sometimes you are completely and blissfully unaware of that moment, sometimes you are so painfully aware you relive it over and over. Life becomes a loop reel of that one second. That one second turns into minutes, minutes turns into hours becoming into days, you end up spending what life you have in a constant battle of what if's, woulda, shoulda and coulda's.

July had always been my favorite time of year, made up of never ending days, night time swims, kids giggling and lazy days at the lake and beach with friends and family. Women's clothes got lighter and smaller, skin became bronzed and everyone had earned the right to be a little lackadaisical.

Danny, Michaels younger brother had become the anchor to reality, seemingly one of the few people Michael had in his life that truly cared lately. Now when Danny showed up at Michaels, most of the time he felt like he was intruding on Michael's cherished moments of self-loathing. He was uninvited to the personal pity party that had become his brother's life.

Brothers though they were, Danny and Michael looked nothing alike. When they were younger Michael used to tease Danny saying that they won him on the pier. It was either Danny or the Plastic Grape Ape doll, and Michael said he had wanted the ape. Danny was blessed with the exotic looks of the extended family, thick black wavy hair, hazel eyes and a dentist's million dollar smile. Almost four inches smaller then Michaels, he was built like a bull. Naturally muscular and agile, his first curl was done with the formula bottle. For all of his strong, overtly masculine physical attributes, he was gentle, understated and compassionate. People, children and even animals were drawn to him. Jilly was just like her uncle. Because of that Michael could never say no to Danny.

Danny went inside the house, unannounced. He found his brother sitting, staring at nothing in particular, a burned out cigarette still in his hand.

"Hey M Man, you gotta get your shit together bro. Poor Dozer should not have to live like this." Danny said this half in jest, half in heartfelt honesty. He proceeded to the kitchen to arm himself with supplies. As he looked around he started clearing debris from the living room into an industrial sized garbage bag in one hand, wiping underneath with a wet rag in the other

Michael continued to stare out the window, barely acknowledging him with a grunt and a nod. He watched as the world went about their business around him. The neighborhood kids are playing on their manicured yards, slipping down the pool slides while moms looked on with cocktails and sunscreen on hand. The flowers this time of year leave a sweet sticky scent that lingers in the air long after the sun has dipped into the Pacific.

I feel like I am watching from the outside, he thought bitterly. Detached, no matter how hard I try to get involved. Even going through the motions seems to be more then I can handle. Barb, my neighbor of eleven years catches me through the window and waves at me, and all I can do is avoid her gaze.

Finally turning toward his brother, the shell of the former man began to speak in a soft defeated voice. "Eyes say so much, and pity is something I have had an eternity of. How many times can I hear hey, how ya doing? Is there anything you need? We are here for you. My personal favorite, you look like hell Michael, are you feeling Ok?"

Danny moved around the room like an ant on a mission while his brother went on. He knew from the tone in Michael's voice he was speaking to no one in particular, and decided that the statement didn't need answering.

"How does one answer these questions? How am I doing? Well, my wife is dead and my kids have been missing for two years. What do I need? Well, thanks for asking. What I need is my fucking family back. Thank you for being here for me. Where are you dear neighbors and acquaintances and ex co-workers when the clock is laughing at me at three o'clock in the morning for the fourth night straight without more then and hour or two of solid sleep? Really, do I look like hell? Sorry, haven't you heard that GQ hasn't taken to the rotting from the gut look yet. Maybe they will, hell it was heroin chic in nineties."

9.

A knock on the door snapped Michael momentarily from the invective narrative with the various demons that had taken up residence in his head over the last two years. Danny was never so glad for an interruption in his life.

Michael stood to answer it. He was well past the point of embarrassment over the state of the house. The stench of a frat house permeated every room. Empty bourbon and scotch bottles lines the counters, cartons of cigarette butts overflowing every half-finished beer bottle. Chinese, Mexican and Pizza containers strewn about, it wasn't like he had been entertaining as of late. Danny hadn't been there long enough to truly make a dent in the rubbish, but God knew he was trying.

Dozer looked up from his permanent spot on the throw rug in front of the fireplace and gave a somewhat aloof grunt and went back to resting. His eyes half open watching every move in the house from under a hooded gaze. Michael opened the door expecting to see another well-wisher or bible beater from the local church they used to attend. Daylight had not been an ally to Michael, so he had avoided it at all costs. Seeing the two men in black suits, shiny shoes, and perfectly cropped hair made Michael feel as if thousands of spiders were crawling over every inch of his flesh. The agents stood at the door, flashing their FBI badges opening a flood gate of emotions he was not prepared to deal with. "Hi." managed to escape his lips as he stepped aside granting the access to the living room.

Watching the men he remembered the one agent from Yosemite. Agent Carbone was different from the typical "cop" types. He was in his early fifties and had never gotten jaded from the shit storms that he had dealt with over his career. He was compassionate and never stopped working to find the kids.

"Agent Carbone, were you just in the neighborhood and decided to pop in to catch up on the latest gossip? I'm sorry. If I had known you were coming for a visit I would have baked a cake and made some tea."

"Mike how ya been? This is Agent Robert O'Neal. Do you have a minute? We need to talk."

Danny came to the door, led Michael to the couch and guided the agents to the cleanest spot in the room. He left the front door open to circulate the air, discreetly turning on the ceiling fan hoping to circulate the fresh air. That did not help defer the tension in the room, thick as molasses and just as uncomfortable. Dozer picked up on this inching himself in between the agents and Michael.

"Mike, I am so sorry." Agent Carbone started the conversation, looking down at the floor, unable to look Michael in the eyes after years of promises he was never able to keep. The words hung in the air for what seemed to be hours.

Michael knew this day would come, but he was not prepared for it in the least. From that instant he was a million miles away as he heard Agent Carbone telling him they have found the remains of his children. At no time are you ever prepared to hear those words.

It's like someone just erased his entire past. Poof, fifteen years of his life had never happened. As though he had never met Merl, never gotten married, never became a father.

Danny moved over and sat on the arm of the couch next to his brother. Unconsciously he wrapped his arm around Michael's shoulder, creating a barrier of protection from the story unfolding, enveloping them. The brothers listened, silent and stoic all color draining rom their faces. The agents looked squarely into their unblinking, unbelieving eyes, telling them that the perp was in custody and that they would be kept apprised of any breaks and how they would be proceeding from here on out.

Agent Carbone and Agent O'Neal stood up and shook Michael and Danny's hands. An oddly polite gesture after the nuclear bomb they just dropped.

"Mike" Agent Carbone lays his hand on Michaels shoulder, "It's over, it's finally over and I am so sorry." Danny thought he caught the agent's eye glass over, just for a split second. The toll of dealing with missing kids and their desperate families bubbled to the surface but just as quickly disappeared into the abyss where all the heartbreak and guilt

and rage bubbled and churned like lava waiting to erupt under the
pressure like a volcano.

10.

The agents pulled away as Michael sat on the couch, stunned and ashen. He was looking at pictures on his side table. Pictures of his perfect family from only 2 years ago, how could so much have changed? Shaking, two years of pent up rage festering like a poison in a cauldron. Two years of guilt for fucking his wife and not protecting his kids, two years of self-hatred and venom for the bastard that did this boiled in his veins, he felt like he was going to explode.

"Ya know somehow, some way I always thought that when my life became shit it would be a test. One of those aha moments that once it passed, I would get my life back on track. Waking up from this nightmare together with my entire family- we would move forward, reconnect, become whole again."

Dozer shifting and landing on top of Mike's feet look at him with his soulful eyes as if he understood every word coming out of his mouth. He sensed the urgency and severity of what had just transpired, and he did everything in his power to console his inconsolable master. He used his body as a shield and pressed his entire one hundred and sixty plus pounds into Michael's legs.

Danny cleared his throat attempting to skirt the sting he himself was dealing with at the moment to be strong for his brother. "You really need to stop man. At least you know now. You knew for a long time, but now, now you have closure."

"Closure? Come again?" Michaels eyes now wide as saucers, skin tightening on his clenched jaw.

Danny was pacing nervously wearing away the carpet under his feet. He was avoiding direct eye contact with any of the mementos in fear of going over the edge. "You can finally put it to rest man. You can start to move on. Don't you get it? Maybe this is a gift, not the curse it feels like."

Michael bent over looking like he was about to get sick, his skin going from sallow gray to a green undertone. He clutched a pillow, kneading it with his sweaty fists as if ready to rip it into shreds. "After Mer, I had hoped that the kids would be living with some religious zealot of a crazy family, all healthy and happy. That they would end up finding me from a computer search at school. They would remember me and dream of coming home to me every night. I would go to sleep visualizing them, what they look like now. Bad haircuts, the awkward phase preteens go through."

"You can't torture yourself like this." Danny kneeled in next to Mike and Dozer on the floor, mindlessly caressing the dog's soft fur to ground him and protect him at the same time.

"I knew that they had each other and that the three of us would eventually have each other again." Michael didn't mention the loss of Merl. He couldn't even bring her into the equation and Danny wanted desperately to broach the subject. Taboo as it was, it was appropriate yet unapproachable.

He swallowed and took the plunge. "Mike, I am so sorry man. It hasn't been a year since Merleigh and now this? Jesus, just talk to me, OK? Just tell me what ya need? I need to do something. Please, just talk to me."

What do I need? Michael contemplated this question for a few seconds. What is it that I need? I need to get my hand around the neck of the bastard who murdered my children and make this mother fucker pay for the past eight hundred or so days of torture he put my family through. I need the chance for retribution and I want to make it crueler, five, no ten, no one hundred times worse for this sick fuck then he made it for them. "I am glad Merl doesn't have to hear that her son and daughter were murdered or how. Not knowing is what killed her. But this would have been worse. My God..." Michael's voice breaking "...why wasn't I there. I don't know if I can tolerate the minutiae of what they must have gone through. I am not sure I want to read the coroner's report. In a way, I was the catalyst for all that has been dark and evil for the past few years. Maybe, just maybe, I was never meant to have the life I had and karma, or the universe or whatever grand fucking scheme made the decision that they were going to right the wrong and my family got run the fuck over in the meantime."

"It wasn't meant to be. There is nothing you could have done man. Things played out. Life sucks and you were caught in the middle of the tempest." Danny pours them each a stiff drink hands a glass to Michal and sits down on the floor cradling Dozer. He needs an anchor and Dozer seems the most logical solution.

"Why didn't I hear them Danny? Or see them, sense them, feel them being taken away?!? What kind of man lets this happen? What kind of father..." Michael knew damn well what kind of man. But there are things that the mind doesn't allow itself to process. Self-preservation for what it's worth.

"Let go and let God. Mike, it's what Merl and the kids would want for you now."

"God? Let God? If there's a God then why, why God, why? What kind of God let's this shit happen. Fuck him and all of the happy do-gooders who want me to turn to him and the fucking church." Mike took a huge gulp of whiskey and spat it across the room. "That is what I think of let God."

Danny, who feared karma more than God himself, was not prepared for this discussion. The superstitious portion of him was not comfortable fucking with fate or taking God's name in that much vane. Attempting to steer this into a safer direction, Danny began "Yeah, well...You can't keep doing this alone man. You need someone or something to help you. You may not want to hear it, but you are not superman".

"Yeah, no, I guess I'm not".

Danny lit a cigarette and took an awkward drink of bourbon. His throat is tight and it is difficult to swallow. "This has been one helluva day."

This poor son of a bitch, what more can he handle? Danny said a silent prayer.   God, give me the guidance to help him, cause right now I got nothing.

Danny pulls out another cigarette and offers it to Michael as he tops off their drinks. Michael starts pacing in front of the back sliding door. Michael starts shaking his head no, "As much as I need it, I'm sticking to the bourbon." Raising his hands defensively, Danny walks up behind Michael and squeezes his shoulder and shrugs, his eyes watering fighting the good fight to hold back tears.

11.

The room was dark, not night time dark but dark like a scary basement or an alley in the wrong part of town. It wasn't just dark from the lack of light, but from the lack of any good. Evil lurked in the corners, dripped down the interior walls, hung in the air like smog over LA. There is a mattress shoved in the corner on the floor in the shadowy room.

Joey is screaming.

"What's happening to him? Why can't I see him? Please God, I'll be good, just let me see my brother, please God, please?" Jilly closed her eyes and prayed the way Danny taught her to when she was nervous, scared or alone.

She remembered an elderly woman from church. One Sunday at an ice cream social the woman had told her that whispered and silent prayers were the ones that God answered first. Jilly remembered how random this advice was at the time. She pondered it for a few moments not knowing what the odd little woman was talking about as she stood in line for her second helping of chocolate chip mint.

Jilly knew now what the woman was telling her, what she was trying to convey. Ironic how moments you thought you forgot come back to you as if they happened only a few seconds ago even years after they initially occur. She wondered if that woman had an evil room of her own. She wondered how many evil rooms there were in the world.

Her angelic face is bruised and dirty. Dried blood flaked in the corner of her mouth. The taste of blood so salty yet sweet made her mouth water and her stomach churn. Her face and eyes so swollen she could only sleep leaning against the wall.

She trusted her Uncle, she even trusted the little old lady at church. She was holding on to hope against hope her prayers were going to be answered. Her mommy and daddy where looking for them, she knew it in her heart of hearts. God won't let her down.

The mattress which she first thought was put there for small comfort has since been turned into a torture chamber. A shadow appears behind her and heavy footsteps come toward her. She inhales sharply as she feels his breath on the back of her neck.

12.

Night time, as the witching hour approaches, the clock blinks 2:36 am. Almost 3:00 am, the mocking of the holy trinity The Father, Son and The Holy Ghost. The three o'clock hour shrouded under the cover of the moon is the time for the night dwellers and demons to be at their most powerful and black magic to be most effective. For us mere mortals it is the time when our subconscious opens the flood gates and deprives us of that sweet deep slumber.

A new night filled with hours of desperation. Michael shot right up as he remembered something. He felt around for his lighter, lit a half smoked cigarette he grabbed out of the ashtray and pulled on his sweats. In the black inkiness he trudged over to his computer. The corner of the room illuminated with the ethereal blue light of the dead screen saver.

He sat down, entranced for a moment by the tip of his cigarette, orange and red, hot and burning, like he once was. He turned on the light on the corner of the desk. It was a Tiffany lamp that glowed with warm, pastel colors from the wisteria stained glass. He never liked that lamp. He always threatened that it was going to break one day by "accident." Merl would grab at him and plead, it belonged to her granny and would one day belong to Jilly. Michael would laugh as his elbow would get dangerously close to the intricate shade. He now sat, caressing the cool glass under his fingers with the care of a museum curator.

He turned his attention to the computer, clicking the mouse to awake his sleeping machine. On the screen was a post-it with a web site his buddy Eric had given him. Michael sat at his computer looking at a post-it, chewing over to go to the site and accept that he needs help or not accept the help of a support group that is the question.

Hesitantly, he typed in www.ElementalChange.com. Apparently the world now didn't just assume but was now validated in its opinion that he was bat shit crazy and in need of some serious help. This so wasn't his cup of Joe. He could only imagine the wackos, weirdoes and lunatics logged in this time of night. He got up and poured himself a Johnny Walker Green and sat back down. The liquor warmed his belly and took the edge off of his apprehension. Another sip and he started typing while looking at pictures of his late family scrolling on a digital frame. His fingers moved effortlessly. He found it easy to open up under anonymity in the safety of his own cloistered world. He began the conversation "I am new to the concept of support groups."

Somewhere in cyberspace, on the other end of a keyboard sat a body by the screen name Elemental. Sitting in a home office Elemental is the man who is the web master, founder and mastermind of ElementalChange.com. He created this site specifically for men who have had experiences with being the victim of violent crimes against their loved ones.

He types, his computer screen flickering showing with chat room chatter. "Welcome. You've come to the right place."

Michael rubs his eyes red. The dark circles from lack of sleep plus his pupils dilating from nicotine, alcohol and lack of light making them look eerily soulless. He catches his reflection momentarily in the glass of the picture frame and is startled to see what is looking back at him. His hand shaking as he types "I just didn't know where else to turn."

"I read your bio. I am so sorry for your loss. We can all relate to the extreme violence and injustices of the world. Tell me, what brings you here to us tonight?"

"I can't sleep. I feel sick. I can't concentrate." Michael seemed to have found the pressure valve. Once he pulled the plug from the dam the words rushed out like water through the drain. This was a welcome release, even if it was his most private thoughts, an admission of weakness IN Michael's mind, from the most intimate space of his being that for the past two years even he has been too uncertain, too terrified to explore.

"That is a natural psycho-physiological reaction to trauma. This is a type of PTSD." Elemental knew that this one needed him. He knew that this was the reason he started this project. He thought it peculiar how the universe worked sometimes.

"What was left of my life is unraveling at a sick and slippery pace and there isn't a fucking thing I can do about it." Michael was surprised at the ease of which he was communicating with this complete stranger, but he was motivated to continue.

As if reading his mind, Elemental's words appeared on his screen, "You are safe here. You are free to express the inner thoughts that haunt you. We all have them. They are torturing you. We can help quiet them, but only by feeling it and revealing it we can heal it. Tell me, how did you find us?" Elementals hands typed with the ease of an author. His fingers so familiar with the keys that they moved over them like an old lover over the body of his bed mate.

"I got your info from a friend I trust. I am not a believer in self-help, new age BS. PTSD and inner voices, I don't know. Thank you for your time. I'm not sure this is for me." Michael felt doubt and fear creeping in, growing inside him and making them at home again.

"We are all here because of the shit that civilization has allowed to roam the streets. These vile bile souled sons of bitches have preyed on our homes, our families, our children. The liberal tree hugging pussies have decided that these scum bags deserve cable TV and down comforters because their mommies didn't love them. So now the societal feces come out of jail a better criminal than when they entered only to continue to rape, torture, mutilate, murder those we love so they can return to get three square, free medical and a place to call home."

Michael looked down at the case report he had yet to open. Memories flashing back to the day he found out the details...

Agents Carbone and O'Neal had returned and were knocking on Michael's door. Michael opened the door stepping back to allow the agents entry. This time he was alone. He didn't have the protection of his brother to balance him.

"We wanted to give this to you personally. The coroner finished the autopsies and…

I am sorry to have to tell you this..." Agent Carbone couldn't even look Michael in the eye.

13.

Joey stood naked, his wrists bound by rags to a metal pole inches away from a hot water heater. A small leak caused years of condensation and rust to mutate into a black hybrid mold that dripped down the side of the pole and soak into the rags.

The room went from bone chilling cold to excruciatingly hot in a matter of minutes, fluctuating wildly all day and all night long. He could barely make out the bloody mattress on floor. He could smell that his sister had been in close proximity, but the lack of light and severe facial beatings had made it hard to see anything that wasn't directly in front of him. Every once in a while he would be exposed to sever spotlights that burned his retina from being in the dark for so long. This left his disoriented and blinded for hours.

He had been given water and some type of sustenance in the mornings, or at least that was his assumption of the time. There was a pan of water. But it was salty, and brutal thirst made it impossible not to drink from which only exasperated him and burned the sores in his mouth and open wounds of his skin.

He heard the door slamming upstairs. The hairs on his body stood on end. The heavy footsteps, the click of the metal dead bolts, by now he knew what ever was coming could only get more sadistic. How much longer will this go on? He knew that if anyone could or would save them, he knew it would be his father. He held onto the slight sliver of hope that his dad would come through that door and take them home.

He closed his eyes and prayed for his daddy to come. Dear God, please let daddy find us. Please let someone save us. Dear God, do you hear me? If you can't, at least help Jilly. God, I am her brother, I can't protect her, but I know you can. Please, ok? For her, if not for me?

"No... Please... no..." Jilly sounded like she was miles away yet right there.

He spotted a pan of sizzling hot oil on a kerosene stove. Hissing and spattering as the oils temperature rose. He felt oil being poured from pan over his skin, even though it was being used on Jilly. Sounds of a young girl's blood curdling screams penetrated the air cutting into him like razor blades. His sisters pain was now his own.

14.

It was a long night, and Michael decided sometime this morning that the day would be best spent sitting on his front steps, smoking cigarettes. Getting some fresh air, a little sun, plus the fact that the stench in his home was starting to make him gag.

Drinking the last sip of his 6th beer, he felt the false pride of completion. It was a good feeling to see that he actually finished something, even if it was a six pack of IPA. Eyeing the bottles lined up next to him he took a deep drag and it hit him, I am that guy. Running his fingers through his greasy hair he started to accept who he was turning into without the slightest regret of the great man he had been in the not so distant past and may still be, somewhere deep inside.

A red pickup pulled up into the driveway, oversized tires and too much chrome for it to do anything but attract attention. Merl used to tease Danny that that truck could be seen from space. She was sure some foreign intelligence thought it was an unnamed star in a far off galaxy; Danny hopped out like a pro and stood at the base of the steps cracking open the first beer from the six pack next to Michael.

"Yo bro, what up?"

"Besides the fact that you have become monosyllabic? It's been five days, thirteen hours and twenty seven minutes since the FBI showed up at my door again. They told me with their stoic, professionalism that my son and daughter were tortured and handed me the report for my reading pleasure. Let's see, what the fuck is up? Just fuckin nothin Bro, just fuckin nothin."

Danny twinges at the retort, but straitens his back, sets his jaw and proceeds with caution. "You look like hell man. Have you slept or eaten anything besides a Sam Adams in the past five days?" The rancid odor coming from Michael was one that pervaded the senses in a NY subway in late August. Danny inhaled sharply as he moved closer to him.

Glaring at Danny Michael snapped back, "I have a great idea, how about you mind your own fuckin business. I really don't need a lecture from my little brother."

"Down tiger, I am just watchin out for ya, dannnng, no need to shoot the messenger!" He reached over his brother and started loading the cardboard with the empty bottles. "This place looks like a war zone. Smells even worse. Because you are my flesh and blood, and because you covered for me with the rents for years, I am going to slip into my cutest little French maid outfit and clean your chateaux Monsieur Mitchell." Danny explained in the worst imaginable French accent he could muster.

A smile escaped from Michael's lips, though it lasted only a split second. It was the first time he let his guard down and that was a good sign.

"I know, I know, sorry, k? It's just... Are you fucking kidding me? THEY had the balls to say I'm sorry. Two years of asking, begging for information and all they can say is I'm sorry, here's the report, bye bye!"

"Come on in and let me call for a pizza. Why don't you go hop in the shower. A little pizza and a hot shower have solved many of the most insidious problems of the world ya know." Smiling that Eric Estrada smile Danny sheepishly opened the door to the house.

Michael stood, a little dizzy from the heat and the beer, he held onto the railing until he got his bearings. Slowly he followed Danny to the kitchen and plopped down on a bar stool. His movements were overly animated, exaggerated. Slurring slightly he began "Standing by, begging for answers as my wife was falling into a narcotic stupor. Deeper, darker, every day and I never bothered to notice. You know what? Those fucking doctors who just kept writing the scripts, Dr. Feelgood and Dr. Iwantyourmoney, they never noticed she was an addict. She was in such a dark place, and I was too busy trying to be a super hero and following every half assed lead I would conjure. Disappearing for days, returning back to where it happened like I could do something the FBI couldn't. "

"Sounds a little like what you're doing right now, man. You just traded places with Merl. Step back and take a good look at yourself. You gotta stop beating yourself up. You think Joey and Jilly bean would want to see their dad like this? Huh? Do you think that you are making them proud by acting the fool? Damn bro, pull your shit together. You had your time to grieve, but you need to take the first step, start to heal, move on already."

Michael nods and looks over at Danny, but he fades away. All he can see is Merleigh leaning against the kitchen cabinets holding the kids' tee shirts to her face, smelling them. She is wearing a ratty tee shirt and sweat pants that are two sizes too big for her. Since the day the kids vanished she stopped acting human.

She is crying but her eyes are dry. The tears have dried up but the pain is more intense every day that passes. Her shoulders heaving as she silently rocks back and forth. Her usually beautiful, glossy blond locks are now oily and slicked back behind her ears. Her face is sunken from refusing to eat. She has been surviving off a solid diet of sleeping pills, antidepressants and anti-anxiety meds. Dark circles formed under her bloodshot eyes now look like they are purple and blue.

Danny helped Michael come back to him, hoisting Michael's arm over his shoulder "Come on my man. Let's get you upstairs, a shower is calling you by name."

Trying to maneuver a drunken Michael is much harder then it looked from the onset. He is quite spry for a beer soaked string bean and Danny wasn't prepared for it. He likened it to what it must be like herding cats soaked with olive oil.

Michael started pounding his fist on the table, standing yet hunched over as if someone has hit him in the stomach. He was screaming no, no, no over and over again. Danny needed help with and for Michael. For the first time Danny was truly scared for his brother.

Repeating the conversation with the agents, "I'm... sorry... they have the balls to say I'm sorry?" Michael grabbed Danny's shirt with his fists, looking at him like a lost child. "What the fuck does that even mean?"

Danny got in Michaels face, "You need to calm it the fuck down, now! You aren't going to accomplish anything if you keep going over what you did and didn't do. What did and didn't happen." He lowered his tone, "Let's just concentrate on today, tomorrow we will think about that and then we will work from there."

Michael was on a rampage. "Do they mean sorry you couldn't stop the mother fucker that did this. Sorry that my wife lost her shit and OD'd?" Michael was yelling, heaving his shoulders, trying to make Danny understand. "Sorry sir, your son and daughter were tortured and nobody cared enough to find them before all that was left was carnage and DNA identifiers? Come on Danny- tell me exactly what the fuck are they sorry for again?"

Danny knew he had to work through it. He also knew that he needed more then he alone could give him. Danny finally got Michael upstairs and into the shower. He went through his closet and lay out clothes that actually had buttons and zippers. " Yo M-man, don't forget to shave, people are starting to think we have found the missing link and that it's alive and well here in The Bay area!"

Michael appeared in the doorway, towel around his waist and a hang-over starting to pound at the base of his skull. He walked over to Danny and put his arm around his little brother's shoulder. The two stood there looking at their reflections in the full length mirror of the closet door.

They were opposite in so many aspects, but seeing them standing next to one another, there was no denying that they were brothers. Blood runs deep. Michael knew he had to start moving forward, not just for the family he lost but for the family he had left.

15.

Eric Berkstrom had been Michael's best friend and partner in crime since they met freshman year in Texas. The two sat next to one another during a frosh seminar and within a week switched roommates and had been yin and yang happily ever after.

Michael got a call from his old friend inviting him to meet up at his firm. Michael wasn't particularly interested in the prospect of going back to the area of his old office. The buildings were within a two block radius of each other. This was no accident, it was purely by design. Michael was a highly respected mechanical engineer at a very large, well respected company with the United States Government as their primary golden goose. The building complex was in the warehouse district if the North Bay, a very unassuming and very secretive building with a million dollar panoramic view of the bay. The public went about their days never knowing what was happening inside the walls of those old warehouses.

After Eric graduated from Columbia top of his Law Class, he passed the New York, California and Washington DC Bar exams without ever breaking so much as the slightest sweat.

He hustled through the ranks at rapid fire speed. The firm had offered him a sign on before he had his diploma in hand. By the time Eric was thirty four he had made senior partner with clients and contacts in every corner of the globe.

Eric made the strategic decision to go from corporate law to personal interest and asset protection. He opened a new office within a few hundred yard of Michael's office, only in a much less discrete building. Michael thought it was overtly ostentatious, but for the group of clients Eric catered to, that was exactly what it needed to be. Due to the fact that Eric was no longer practicing the corporate facet of the law, the non-competes he had signed in blood no longer held water.

Eric happily gathered his clients who followed this pied piper directly to his new firm which bore his name. Two years later Eric hired corporate lawyers who cannibalized his previous employer's client list to the point of nearly driving the firm to extinction. All very nasty but all very legal and Eric did it all with a smile, a twinkle in his eye and a shake of a perfectly manicured hand.

Admiration for each other was a large keystone of the basis of Eric and Michael's relationship. Michael admired the consummate professionalism and cool demeanor that Eric possessed. Eric admired the fire in Michael's belly the passion and genuine likability that made everyone fall head over heels for him.

As Michael approached he stood outside for a moment collecting his thoughts. The smell of the Bay brought back some brighter times, memories that had escaped him for the past two years. He looked at the dual story brass and mahogany doors with the letters Berkstom & Assoc. above. He never thought he would need to summon courage to see his best friend, yet he had been avoiding him since he found out about the kids. Well, this time was as good as any to face Eric.

Michael walked through the palatial doors to find the receptionist surrounded by marble and lush fabrics looking impassively at the computer screen. She was a 20-something beautiful Asian woman dressed in a body-hugging red Chanel suit, conservative high fashion. Shoes Louis Vuitton's barely worn, red gel nails perfectly manicured and her voice has the perfect inflections as she spoke like being wrapped in warm caramel. Michael thought to himself she was one step from Vogue or two steps from being the First Lady or a possible demonic under lord. Polish like that does not come cheap or easy.

The receptionist looked up and saw Michael walking toward her. She smiled warmly and rose from her desk. "Mr. Mitchell, Mr. Berkstrom is ready to see you. Please follow me."

"My pleasure" he responded. As Michael did so, he enjoyed the view thinking to himself, this is definitely my pleasure. They walked through what felt like a mile of marble tiled halls with fine art from Eric's private collection up lit by crystal sconces to the elevators. The elevator doors opened to a glass encasement that rode up the outside of the building. Michael followed the receptionist into the glass car, as the doors closed behind him he was caught off guard, the doors closing behind him. The views of the bay were breathtaking. Looking out on a clear day you could see the Golden Gate Bridge and the Bay Bridge.

Michael's favorite time to look out was at dusk. The ships and building surrounding the water seemed to twinkle like stars with the last of the day's sun light illuminating them from behind. He stood still as a manikin, letting memories of the hundreds of times he had taken this ride flood back into his conscious, washing over him like a cool shower on a blistering summer's afternoon. The elevator door opened directly into Eric's office, startling Michael back to reality.

"Michael, come on in." Eric stood up and clasping Michaels hand with both of his. "Here, sit down. How are you holding up buddy? You look like Hell!"

Eric had maintained an aura of youth through the years. His eyes lit up when he spoke, his skin still smooth and dewy as a teenager, despite the crow's feet creeping in at their corners adding just the right amount of age to command respect. His hands soft to the touch, when he shook your hand he adding the prefect amount of pressure asserting authority yet his left hand automatically grabbed your shoulder and made you believe you were part of a secret club only for the chosen few. As he spoke he leaned into you as if sharing a secret. His voice has the tone of a tenor, slightly graveled from the eighteen hour a day schedule he has maintained since college. Ninety percent work, but when Eric played he knew how to play with the big dogs. He somehow managed to balance that subtle maturation needed in his line of work with the youthful, almost playful characteristics of a tiger cub. The key to his success is that he poises the two with an undercurrent that his adulations could turn at the drop of a hat and he would be as menacing as a king cobra and just as deadly under the right circumstance.

"That seems to be the general consensus, thanks for pointing it out." Michael could not argue with Eric, nor could he deny the accusation. Eric was like blood, after Danny, he was the only person in the world Michael had that he could trust with his life. Michael looked at Eric and shrugged his shoulders, not wanted to expand the crevice of this conversation any deeper than it had been already.

Eric walked over to the window, the city has started to illuminate with the sun setting to the west mixing with the manmade glow of electric light gave the bay the impression that it was glowing like the light of a candle. He held up a bottle of Glenmorangie 18 Years Old pouring two neat into crystal glasses. "I know how hard this has been on you."

Michael takes the scotch from Eric slowly sipping the golden liquid allowing the taste settle in his mouth. He swallows feeling work its way down from the back of his throat to his chest into his gut. He looks out over his city wistfully with pain permeating his face. "Let's just say it hasn't been easy."

"I have something we need to discuss. I didn't think it was appropriate to speak to you over the phone about it. I know that Merl wasn't what you would call stable toward the end. No disrespect intended. That said I hope you realize how much she loved you and the kids. The only thing that girl ever wanted was to make sure her family was taken care of."

"Eric, I get it, I really do. I know this had been a bitch slap for everybody, but she was my wife. She left me to deal with this crap on my own. I know who I married. I know what kind of mother, wife and woman she was. I am not really sure why you are doing this, but…" Again, he trailed off taking a large gulp, allowing the silence to hang in the air like a loose electric wire. Both men know the game, he who spoke first lost, but this time, one of the few times, Michael was going to hold his ground until Eric cracked.

Eric looked Michael in the eye, holding the gaze a few second longer than normal. Typical Eric using power play nuances. Michael had known him long enough that he had become hyper sensitive to the games he played even if Eric played them subconsciously. "That's not why I asked you here, Mike. I am not defending her. She is not on trial, but she was a client."

"Please forgive me if I am blaming her for being so fuckin' selfish, so fuckin' weak. What the hell did she need you for? We were doing well, but certainly not up to the canons of Berkstrom & Assoc."

"Mike, she was stronger then you know. She was also a shrewd business woman. One thing you need to realize, that no matter who you are, no matter how strong, educated, or prepared you think you are to face life's battles, there will always be something or someone out there that will be the stronger, smarter, better equipped or armed and you will end up on the losing end. Nobody gets out of this life without bringing a knife to a gun fight at least once. Unfortunately, in Merls situation, she happened to lose to an opponent without a face or a name. It was the furtive of not knowing that killed her. The unknown was her silver bullet. The point, my old friend is that it was her kryptonite, not yours. You need to go down your own path, do not follow in her footsteps."

"Yeah, well I am not destined to OD, thanks for worrying." After he sat silent, looking at everything in the office except Eric, being a loose cannon was easier and easier with every encounter and Michael was becoming an expert at it.

Eric allowed the awkward silence to fill every crevice of the room until this time Michael broke it. "Are we done here?"

He was getting emotional the scotch breaking down his shielding walls. Emotions are starting to run high. Eric notes the shift yet sits still, like a hawk eyeing its prey from far above.

16.

Michael looks over to Eric. Memories of the two from when they shared a room in college started playing in his mind like a favorite film. He was intimate with the scenes and knew each line by heart.

Playing football in the quad, frat parties, cram sessions, bar crawls and the death of Mike's mom. Flash forward to Eric at Jilly's baptism, holding his Goddaughter during the ceremony and the look on his face as she spit up all over the front of his Paul Stuart Suit. They had a history they had a bond there was no denying that.

Michael's hands were shaking, his voice beginning to crack. "I owe you man. For being there when I was on top of the world then when my world went to shit. I've been easy to dodge. People either overcompensate when a tragedy strikes or they avoid you at all costs. If it isn't easy or mapped out most people can't deal. You and Danny were there. You two have always been there for us, now me. " His voice trailed off the nostalgia that usually comes from old age hitting him unexpectedly.

"There's nothing to thank me for. I'm not sure if you realize that we are friends, hell, minus the DNA I would go as far as to say you are my family. That's what we do. No strings attached. Come on Mike, what're you doing? Where are you going?"

"You know, for a long time people thought I had something to do with it. Something to do with the kids, then something to do with

Mer…" Michael stopped short of her name, taking a long drink. He finally felt the need to explain, to try to sort everything out. "And especially after Mer passed away, the media, the neighbors, even that sleazy guy at the gas station..."

"Human nature buddy, don't take it personally."

He looked down at his shoes, trying not to break. For some reason Eric had a strange effect on him. Michael was an expert at cloaking his emotions, but there was something in Eric's eyes that brought them to the surface, seeping up like crude oil through sand and soil, ugly, slick raw and unprocessed.

"At least the bastard who did it is locked away. He admitted guilt, forewent a trial. It must bring relief to have some closure, some form of justice." Eric was leaning over Michael like a father to a son. The scent of Ambre Topkapi lingered long after Eric had applied it, a definite step above the Drakkar Noir they used to bath in as freshmen over twenty years ago. Subconsciously a half grin came over Michael's face as the faint memory flashed, both disappeared as quickly as they appeared.

"Spoke like a true lawyer. He set the stage. He knew exactly what he was doing."

"You can live without the media circus of a trial. Being a lawyer, I usually am against not having one's day in court, but in this case Mike, it was the only way." Eric knew what the media could do to a family in turmoil, and he was hell bent to make sure that never happened to his friend.

17.

Michael relives the day they decided to go on vacation. It is a day that he seems doomed to repeat until the day he dies. Like any other day, he was dressed in his suit, tie slung over his shoulder. He walked in the door with a pizza, Merleigh and Jilly and Joe were all seated at the table. He plopped the pizza down in the center of the kitchen table, turning and grabbing a beer in the fridge all in one expertly choreographed move.

"Dinner of the kings for my lady, lass and lad." Renaissance iterations were never his strong point, but he tried his best. He flinched as he remembered bending down putting his arms round each of the kids. He tactically centered himself in the middle for his favorite group bear hug.

Merleigh grabbing his beer and taking a man sized gulp. Blowing the curl away from her eyes, the one blond chunk of hair had a nasty habit of wanting to drop in her face no matter how much styling product, flat irons, or whatever else in her arsenal of beauty products she used. Michael found it delicious and she found it to be the bane of her existence.

"Dinner of what for whom? Do us a favor sire, when you climb down out of that ivory tower, may I hold court? I want to discuss something."

Doing his best impersonation of her or Minnie Pearl he replied in a female sing-song voice. "I want to discuss something." Returning to his normal tone, "Those words have caused panic and fear in mankind since the dawn of time."

"Really?" She could get up in arms faster than the wind could shift and just as easily return to park. "We need some QT Mike. Ya know, real family time, maybe meals that call for utensils."

Even their arguments were somehow light. This discussion caused the kids to start giggling while grabbing at the soda and napkins. The TV was blaring in the background with something from the discovery channel on.

"You know I am up to my ass in alligators at work Mer. Every time I turn around someone else needs a piece of me. I can't just pick up and leave." Michael was adamant. He hated to be ambushed, especially in front of the kids.

"Can't you break away from work for a few days, baby?" purring, with that little sensual pout that usually melted him like a hot knife in butter.

Michael kneeled down grabbing Dozer by the chin and hiding behind him, both giving Merleigh huge puppy eyes.

Undeterred Merl bulldozed full steam ahead. "I found the cutest little cabin, right in Yosemite. They take pets and…"

"When did you become a woman of the wild?"

Merleigh answered with her infamous eye roll. This move was perfected during their engagement. As plans were rolling along, everything he had any input on, out came the roll. Grooms cake? Roll. Maroon colors? Roll. A&M stadium themed reception? Roll & huff.

Persistence was not just an attribute, it was her weapon. "Jilly and Joey will be in high school and won't have one memory of us on a family vacation together. Is that something you are willing to live with? Is that something you want on your conscious, causing thousands of dollars and hours of therapy for our kids?" She was spreading it on thicker than her cream cheese icing.

"When did you get the Ph.D. in guilt after marriage or motherhood? Was this one of those suspicious extracurricular activities you had Eric tutoring you in?

Merleigh went over the kids, looking at Michael sideways. "Oooh, hey guys, remember the time we went to Vancouver and we sent Daddy a post card? Hey, y'all remember when we went back east to see Auntie El and Skyped with Dad? Ahhh good times."

As if on cue the three got on their knees, hands clasped pleading "Pleeeease? You promised!"

"Waylaid in my own home come on now, where is the love? This is what I call quality right here, right now." The memory of that statement made Michael wrench.

Merleigh was a skilled negotiator, rebuttal after rebuttal. Rapid fire. "Quality? Glad you're the one who gets to decide what quality time is and what's not. You're the master of the mansion."

"Ouch. Settle down now." Michael knew this could turn ugly, and he really wanted to avoid it at all costs.

"If it wasn't for us you'd live with garbage-packed from floor to furniture, and only use the stove for storage!" Michael thought to himself, if she could see me today and know just how prophetic that statement was…

"Who will pay for these five-star dining experiences like what we've got tonight if I am not at work? By the way, you know I am up for Dad of the Year and Master of the Mansion is one of the categories. How quickly you forget that I was nominated by Dozer?" Pointing to the pooch on the rug in front of the sink snoring.

The three attack him, holding his arms, legs, bear hugs, importuning him, pleading. "Uncle, Uncle! I give!" Animated and goofy, he had been swept up in the moment. In his best partial pirate caricature he gave them what they wanted to hear. "I thinks me may be able to clear sometime before the end of the month. Mer, go for it! Great outdoors, watch out, you ain't seen nothin' yet! Hey, do you think Vincenzo's delivers there too?"

18.

"Hey, you OK? I thought I lost you there for a minute." Eric sat down in front of Michael. A look of genuine concern washed over his friends face.

Michael rubbed his forehead. Standing up he was disoriented, the room was spinning. He walked unsteadily over to the wall of windows overlooking the Bay. He stood looking out with his back partially to Eric as he grappled with what had just happened.

"No, reality hasn't hit yet. It's all so bizarre, like I am watching this movie in my head. I want to walk out. Stop the reel. But something is forcing me to remain in my seat."

"Did you get a chance to look at the website I sent you? I know you aren't an aficionado of self-help BS, but..."

"Actually I went on last night."

"Well, what did you think?"

Michael turned to Eric locking in on his eyes. "Yeah, about that, it was different. I like the no personal identification rules. I'm still a bit skeptical, but it felt good to vent." As he answered he never broke his gaze yet Eric knew that Michael was somewhere else.

"Glad to hear it. Give it time. I know it will do some good." He was a master of body language. Arms open, smiling, all-encompassing yet not overpowering. Michael knew the gestures were deliberate, and after all these years he found it repulsive. He returned back to his drink, eager for the last mouthful of scotch to wash away the distrust that was edging in.

"You said that I was lucky to avoid the media circus. Well my friend, hate to break it to ya that hasn't exactly been the situation. Even without a trial, the media has been all over me like white on rice since they identified Jilly and Joe."

"Do you need me to file a restraining order? Do you want to file stalking charges? The paparazzi are parasites, but I do have some leverage. The great state of California, thanks to our LA comrades, has actually done something right when it comes to privacy laws."

"No. I just feel like a bottle of soda that has been left in a hot car than dropped. Any second I am might explode on the first person who attempts to have me open up."

"Natural, you are not the first person to feel this way. I know you need some release. You can't keep it locked up like you do."

"I walk around the house and I think I hear them laughing and bantering, I catch a shadow. I could swear they are still running around." Michael had moved back to his seat. Actually he felt more relaxed right now then he had in months. Maybe it was the scotch, maybe it was being with an old friend or maybe it was that time was actually healing the wounds, but whatever it was he was grateful for these few minutes of lucidity.

"You need to stop punishing yourself. Don't own it because it's not your fault. It's like you had that entire part of your life erased. I don't know…"

"Can we not go there, K?"

"K. Sorry. Moving forward is what Merl and the kids would want."

"No, I think what they would want is to live the life they were supposed to have lived. "

"Snap back pal. Here and now. That's where you need to be. Here, now."

Totally ignoring Eric's last statement he continued on. The great Eric, controlling his domain unintentionally set Michael off again. "What they would've wanted is to not have their string of time cut by some psychopath's blade. One step at a time, one day at a time. Time heals all wounds. Just give it time. How bout you fuckin try it. Tell me how the book ends."

Eric Grabbed Michael by the shoulders, "Take it down a notch." He commanded a monotone voice that was a fusion of best friend, psychologist, and coach on game day.

"Eric, I wish I could take back every time I was tired and demanded that they quiet down, that I screamed get to your room, I've had enough. Well, I guess I am lucky... I never have to worry about rambunctious kids or a needy wife again."

"I know it's still pretty raw. You have to move on."

"Every once in a while I get a VIP pass to the pity party held at cry me a river and it's hard to leave."

"Nice place to visit, but trust me you don't want to live there.'

"I'm not, at least not as much. The site you suggested has been helping to get some distance."

'Glad to hear it. I didn't mean to jump your shit like that. I just want you to realize you have a life to live."

'It sucks. That site though, man, it's good to know that there are people out there who have gone through it, come out the other side. We may be scarred, maybe a bit broken..."

"Glad to hear you are starting to accept some support. That is one fuck of a weight to carry on your own. No man can walk this path by himself. You do know that Danny and I are here for you, but we are too close to give you totally unabashed answers. We are ancillary parties so we won't ever truly understand where you are coming from."

19.

Jilly sat motionless, sobbing quietly, petrified to make a sound in case he hears her. She is cold, lonely, clinging to her one wish. Silently she prays to a God she isn't sure of. "I want my Daddy."

A shadow is casted on a decaying brick wall of a man thrusting his hips and grunting. She knows something is happening, but she can't make out what it is. She catches sight of the back of a hand moving in a violent downward back slap motion. The shadow is huge, and she has felt the scorn of that hand. Suddenly the sharp sound, a whack, then another, then another, skin on skin, unmistakable brutality. A muffled inhale and a defenseless yelp the only sounds breaking the silence of the dark. Whack… whack…whack. Joey was in pain and she was helpless.

"Joey?" she whispers under her breath hoping that her voice would carry to his ears, "Noooo no no no no no." Rocking back and forth, grabbing her knees into her chest. She balled up smaller and smaller, praying that she becomes invisible to the monster. Kione appeared in the doorway. "You called?"

Blood spatters in the air and lands on a cinderblock wall. Stinging from the aftershock of the electric cord on her raw skin she turns to the wall. He leaves her in silence.

Joey is holding in the pain, she hears his labored breathing. She watches the shadows and knows exactly what Kione is doing. She wishes she could stop him. She wishes she could help her big brother.

As he finishes, she watches his shadow arching his neck back. She looks away only to see a young boy's underwear piled on the ground soiled and blood stained. She knows they are Joey's.

Kione looks at his reflection, his face partially reflected in the mirror. He can only see his eyes and forehead. He continues looking down at his hands, washing off over a grime filled sink. The chipped porcelain and hard water stains mixed with dry blood left a deep ginger stained ring at the water line.   The feeling of entitlement mixed with the piquancy of victory. Today was one of his better days.

20.

Eric had a very long day. His clients seemed more demanding than usual as if that is even possible. Michael sat here, looking to him for support and encouragement. He needed to be that friend. He owed it to him, yet part of him just wanted Michael to get on with his life. He wanted to scream at him to stop being such a pussy. Man the fuck up. His patience was running very thin, and he had to fight his own inner battles to be supportive as he had to be.

"Well, onto the business at hand. Mer came here and had her will redone right before you left for Yosemite. She was scared something would happen. Predictive? Maybe. We'll never know." As he rambled through the turn of events he handed Michael a substantial check. Michael's eyes went wide at the paper in his hand. His grip tightens not with gratitude but rage.

"Is this meant to be some sick consolation prize?" All of a sudden Michael starts to speak in a game show host voice eerie, maniacal, out of body speaking in the third person. "Mike, come on down! You've lost everything in your life of value -congratulations, here's your prize!

Eric tensed his shoulders, putting the desk between him and his friend. "I thought this would go smoother."

"Eric you can take this fucking check and burn it, eat it, shove it up your ass until it tickles your tonsils for all I care. I don't need the money, I need my family back." He turned and crumpled the check, tossing it into the trash. He goes to take a long swig from the empty glass and throws it against the marble tile floor. The crystal ringing as it exploded into thousands of shards embedding themselves into the Persian rug and the crevices of the tile.

"Relax Mike. It's just business. I'm the executer and the accidental OD then the kids. I had a few loop holes to close before I could give this over to you." He ignored the outburst as if it never occurred.

Michael did the same. "Thank you ever so much for fucking with my head. Just what the doctor ordered."

Eric grins. This had always been his tell. When he wanted to cover up his emotions or when he had something to hide the Cheshire grin appeared. "Not exactly the reaction I expected. I am an officer of the court. I am in no way in the mind-fucking business. You can check the sign on the front of the building." Smooth, situation averted.

Mike gets a halfcocked smile despite himself. This roller coaster has to stop. The constant highs and lows are exhausting him. He needs help.

"Mer had a trust set up."

"I never knew.'

"She was a smart lady. She had the foresight to know grief makes people unstable, so she had a safeguard built in. She was worried about avalanches, earthquakes and snake bites. She even cursed the NatGeo Channel for her misgivings about the trip. She said…"

21.

Merleigh walked into Eric's office dressed in NYDJ's and a light blue blazer. She sat down in one of Eric's brushed leather chairs as if it was her office and he was there to see her. She has innocence wrapped in confidence, a certain sex appeal that she either was the master of or she was totally unaware of. Either way, she was dangerous. This was a very pleasant break to an otherwise monotonous day.

"Eric thanks for seeing me. I know you think I'm crazy, but stuff like this happens all the time. I need to know that my family will be OK if anything ever happened to one of us."

"Looks as if you did most of the work for me. This is very well thought out. Did you have this drawn up before you came to see me?" He was always full of compliments, saying the right things to the right people at the right time. "I don't want to know." She shook his head sheepishly smiling to show off his dimples. "Of course, I can set this up for you. I'm not sure what you are so worried about though".

"I know, that damn NatGeo channel and 20/20 on demand. Too much TV not enough sleep."

22.

Michael now sitting in the same chair as Merleigh laughs halfheartedly.

"Mike, you had one helluva lady." Eric looks at Mike, wistfully remembering the trio in the college days and then when he found out the two were engaged. He felt guilty. The jealousy he hid for so many years over what they had built together was so foolish now. He walked slowly over to the garbage, picked up the check and ironed it flat with the palm of his perfectly manicured hand. He refolded it and places it into Michael's shirt pocket.

"I... I... I am sorry Eric." Michael's voice was barely audible. He grabbed Eric's wrist, "I had no idea. There was so much we never said. I always dismissed her. I was always too busy, always had more important things to do."

'That's life. It can get in the way of living."

Mike let out his breath in a long slow exhale through pursed lips while contemplating on just how many levels that statement rang true.

"You never know what you got 'til it's gone. Jesus Christ, I hate those words. Hey, you know that movie with Jack Nicholson?"

"Which one?" Eric shook his head no, then in a moment of recollection, "Do you mean that Marine movie."

"Yeah Jack was spewing something about wanting but not being able to handle the truth. The truth is an ugly bitch. He can have her. I don't want her. I can't handle her. I wish I could just pay her and tell her to go home."

With that hanging in the air, Eric dials his secretary. He spoke into the speaker phone "Hold my calls and clear my calendar for the rest of the day."

"Yes Sir, is everything alright?" Even on the speaker she had the low throaty tone of a pro.

Eric hangs up on her before answering the question. Squaring his shoulders he rubbed his hands together turning to Michael with that devil may cay expression that Michael knew so intimately. "Ready? I am all yours, and from this moment on. You my friend are one lucky bastard to have me free of charge." with emphasis being on the word me.

Michael and Eric entered a pub with an outside bar that was built on pilings over the Bay. Filled with longshoremen, fishermen and dock workers, it was a place where nobody knows your name and nobody cares. No one asks you anything except who you are rooting for, what you want to drink and if you saw the game last night.

23.

On the national news Senator Riley is giving a campaign speech. "California's prison overcrowding is so severe that roughly thirty-five percent of the inmates reside in cells designed for a tenth of the population. Our prisons have classrooms, gyms, and cable TV and even laundry facilities. The felons treat our prisons like a summer camp! There is no incentive to stay out of prison. College courses, computer access, conjugal visits?"

He is of a non-identifiable ethnicity, A-typical politician that covers his smarminess with the constructs passion. The years are not being kind to him, and no amount of makeup can cover the damage from years of alcohol abuse and womanizing. For some inconceivable reason, the press loves him. They hang on every word as if it was gospel.

The front of every newspaper headline reads of prison overpopulation and show pictures of the California prisons, prisoners in the yard, dog pile fights. The CDCR (California Department of Corrections and Rehabilitation) as the locals lovingly call it has become the poster child for prison reform. The citizens are tired of the revolving door and allowing the most heinous of the criminals to be set free due to overcrowding and dirty politics.

Outside the steps of the CDCR in Sacramento the press conference is still going on, reporter's cameras flashing and news microphones shoved into the politicians face just out of camera's scope.

Senator Riley mocks outrage. "The insanity must stop! The state's inmate population is projected to top 200,000, not counting juvenile offenders, resulting in more violence and a higher deficit of funds. I promise you prison reform is the top of my agenda!" He pounds fist on podium heatedly and continues, "I promise to take back our state and reinstate the rights of the innocent and victim over those of the deviant persuasion."

Angola, Louisiana State Penitentiary. A man is getting out of a black Escalade. He walks with a purpose, his black boots hitting the dusty parking lot leaving a low cloud of dust in his wake. He avoids the direct light of the spotlight. Looking up, mosquitos and bugs the size of humming birds fly toward the light of the bulbs.

The warden is an obese, sweaty, pock-marked complexioned 50-year-old man in a uniform one size too small speaking in a slow Louisiana drawl.

He removes his hat to show a scar running down the side of his bald bulbous head. "Suh, I have been around a long time. I just can't do that. Not only is it unethical, but it is certainly illegal. I didn't get elected twenty-seven years ago and win every election since by being part of the immoral, pseudo-criminal persuasion."

The warden leads the man to a back quadrant long ago abandoned since the murder of 4 officers by a prison uprising.

"Sick fucks I tell ya, sick sumofabitches fucking each other, acting like pussies when they're on the wrong end of a gang bang or beat down." The warden's honesty is refreshing.

"Earlier in the week the prisoners gang-raped a female guard. It had been especially violent. They tore her from stem to stern. She was so traumatized she couldn't speak. She is in the hospital now. Doctor's think she may never be right in the head agin even if she does heal physically. Happened in the showers. Not really sure, some're sayin tha it may have been from the inside. She just got pushed up for a promotion. howeva they say, it shudn't go down like that."

He looks out over his kingdom. The men were yelling, screaming with night terrors, real or imagined. He could hear the sounds of bodies slamming against the bars, and it was music to his ears. Even in the dead of night the temperature is hovering well near eighty. The heat oppressive and the humidity wrapped around the throat like a noose, tightening the hangman's knot.

"One minute they is sweet as mam's pie, next minute they're bragging about rapin' little guls and atrocities tha'd rot your soul if ya's hear what they did. Tha muhney would cerr-rtanly help meh keep my budget in line for the upcoming elections. Suh, you want 'em you can 'ave 'em. Hell, suh, I'll give you a two fur if it'd please ya. Bon Ton Roulette."

Near the loading docks, behind the cinderblock walls and double barbed wired gates. A prisoner walks hands cuffed at the base of his spine, a gun to the base of his hooded head. The hooded inmate is shoved into the rear of a black escalade under no more than the light of the moon.

24.

Somewhere off the coast of Guyana is a private Island. The natural beauty is breathtaking. The azure colored waters lap the rocky cragged coast.

Smoke rose off of the side of the foot hills. The smell of burning wood and wet earth permeated the air.

A low sound of heavy machinery became blurred by the sound of the sea and the wind.

25.

Attica, New York, the prison is one of the top ten most dangerous in the USA specializing in inmates with disciplinary problems from other facilities. With midnight only a few minutes away outside the prison is man getting out of a black Escalade. His black boots slosh through muddy puddles on cracked parking lot of the prison. He nods at the guard holding the door, he is expected.

'I have spent my entire career upholding the law. My pop was a cop my grand-dad was a cop too. My family is the reason half of these mother fuckers are in here in the first place. I have seen them come and go and come back again. Different names, different faces, each year a little more sadistic, a little more perverse."

Warden Eli Finch is a typical northeastern wannabe cop. He tried, oh how he tried to become one of New York's finest, but that damn psych test, he was sure is was skewed now for those fucking foreigners. He still proudly wears a cop styled mustache with a military haircut. Poor man can't be taller than 5'5. His overly shined shoes overly starched uniform prove that no matter how hard he tries, he will never be enough.

Sweat beads started to form on his forehead as he looked at the cash sitting inches away from him. He tugs at his collar, staring lecherously as if the money were underage pornography. He's biting his nails incessantly to the nubs, spitting them out as he continues in his mousy cartoon voice. "I am not getting any younger. I have given most of my life and part of my soul to this cesspool. The only thing I have done is educate the next generation of scumbags to be better criminals. I put 'em in solitary so they can store their shit up and throw it in our face when chow time comes. Fuckin' animals! What I'd give to bring the firing squads back, ya know? Do unto others, like the bible says, eye for an eye. Mother fuckers get a hard on thinking up the next drug induced, soulless, wretched idea. Fuck 'em, I wish I could light a match and sell tickets to watch em burn. Shit -- they're gonna burn one way or another... I might as well help."

Minutes later the silhouettes of men in shackles show on the exterior of the prison walls, moving like an animated movie. The inmates are hog tied, hooded and gagged, forced into the back of the very same Escalade as the others.

26.

Another top ten day off the coast of Guyana. The morning sun rises over a tropical island. Approximately one hundred laborers are working on a wilderness lodge. Glass and wood are the primary materials beings constructed at the moment. They work like machines. The rhythmic pound of the hammer, the clank of hammer against nail seems to set the pace for the men. The far off shout of instructions, the roar of a back hoe, encompassed by dense jungle surroundings set the scene for the day ahead. The combination of sounds from nature in the rainforest and the constant drone of man-made sounds from hammers have a primal, hypnotic beat. Farther into the jungle wires and cameras being installed hidden among the flora.

27.

It's the witching hour, three a.m. and a man is getting out of a black Escalade. His black boots hitting a steaming hot parking lot leaving imprints of the boot heel in the black top. The heat from the day permeates the tar.

Warden Carlton P. Bryce is one very uptight very young light skinned black man. They say everybody has a twin and his would be Mayor Corey Booker from Newark, NJ. They say image is ninety nine percent of the game and he was gonna fake it til he makes it. His perfectly shaved head, hazel eyes wide with feigned interest, his suit costing him more than he makes in a month salary, no detail ignored. Even his nails are perfectly manicured, his Ferragamo shoes shined to perfection.

"Welcome to San Quentin State Prison, California." He extended his hand for a shake but the man only stood staring, wordless in reply. An uneasy silence filled the room, but Warden Bryce quickly took care of that. He was in charge here, and he was in no way going to be intimidated in on his playground. He was the only bully in this sandbox. "I received your proposition. Although I understand the relevance and the benefit to our community, as I like to think of it, there is really no way I could condone such an action. Morally, ethically, and spiritually I just don't see a way I could agree.'

A note with a bank account number is slipped across the table magnifying the silence. Warden Bryce types in the number into his iPad and his demeanor seems to unlimber. A genuine smile crosses his face. "To my detriment at times, I've been too quick to make decisions without always weighing the pros and cons. Now that I have all of the facts available to me, I am starting to see how this could be a mutually beneficial relationship. This may morally and spiritually be for the greater good of my men. Exposure to those unresponsive to therapy and rehab is very bad for morale."

The Warden smiles thinking about the week he has had. The showers in prison can be a place of spiritual cleansing. Warden Bryce's officers are tasing the testicles of problem inmates there while the water increases the electric currents. From what he has learned word on the block is there are gang bangs in the showers. Yesterday another dead inmate was found lying in a pool of blood. The best part of his week is his tutorials with the youngest men. Hopefully they will learn their place and not cause problems here. He leans back in his chair, grabbing the back of the youngest inmates head receiving oral sex while praising the lord and his work.

"I concur, we have ourselves a deal."

The sun is starting to light the horizon with a light green aura through the smog and fog. Shackled and hooded inmates are being beaten with jimmy sticks on the back of their knees before they are thrown into the rear of the waiting Escalade.

28.

The lodge is coming along nicely. Cameras are being installed in the trees. Listening devices hidden in the flora. Hundreds of automatic weapons on a flatbed are being off loaded and secured into the outbuilding. The speakers are designed to blend into the dirt below. Every inch of the island can be seen from the main building, if not by design then by electronic surveillance. Keep in mind this is my island oasis, my Shangri-La.

Yet, one can never be too careful, I had to hire US retires military snipers to cover the perimeter, making it impenetrable and militant. Although I see no particular use for them, I also have over a dozen teams of Caucasian Shepherds trained in Siberia along with their handlers. I have planned every aspect meticulously. It is simple really. For every action there will be an equal or greater reaction. I am looking forward to the reaction from the action of erecting my vision.

29.

Jilly and Joey have their hands tied, prong collars around their necks and are gagged in the back of an old sedan, windows heavily tinted. They watch from afar as their father buries their mother.

Kione smiling and singing The Doors as if he were on a family outing,

"Oh, moon of Alabama
We now must say goodbye
We've lost our good old mama
And must have whiskey, oh, you know why
Well, show me the way
To the next little girl
Oh, don't ask why
Oh, don't ask why
Show me the way
To the next little girl
Oh, don't ask why oh, don't ask why
For if we don't find
The next little girl
I tell you we must die
I tell you we must die
I tell you, I tell you I tell you we must die"

Staring at Jilly through the rear view mirror, even at this tender age she could see the unnatural yearning in his eyes and feel the smell the sweet mint of his breath.   She could only male out his mouth or eyes at one time, never his entire face. He feels genuinely content for the first time in years. Eyeing his little darlings in the back seat, watching the spectacle unfold outside, and knowing he was the catalyst for all events gave him a sense of being. He coos into the rear view mirror "My darlings, that's your mother in that hole. The dirt's being thrown on 'er. She killed herself. Now, don't you worry, it is all your fault, but I forgive you."

Giggles gleefully he reaches behind him and back hand Joey so hard one of his teeth fly across the car. In a second he is silent, his eyes deaden, "If I see one tear from either of you, you will be in that box next to that cunt, do you understand?

Minutes feel like hours, Joey sees familiar faces, he wants to scream, he wants to escape, but he is bound and gagged. He can't even reach his sister. The few feet might as well be miles. He can't hear her at all, he wonders if she stopped breathing.

"We lost our dear old mama…" He smiles an angelic smile, soothing and safe is his voice juxtaposed against the words that fall out of his mouth, "She's dead, thanks to you. Your father made her do it so he could be free of any memories of you. I am sure if she could she would thank you."

The music changes and so does he. "Ave Maria" plays in the background. He's becoming agitated as the tension begins to thicken the air. He adjusts the rear view mirror as he looks again in at Jilly. Now his voice is a low growl, "You little slut, did you hear me?" He grabs the steering wheel, knuckles turning white with rage. "You really are worthless."

Joey can no longer contain himself, he urinates in his pants. The acidic smell of ammonia permeates the vehicle. "You little fucking Nancy. You sick little bastard. You can't protect your sister because you're a little faggot. You like it when she screams don't cha? You are a twisted little fuck, piss ant. Can't even control your own piss and people say you're a genius? You are a stupid, useless wart on the cock of a pig. Do you hear me piss ant?"

As the coffin is lowered into the ground and the crowd starts to dissipate, people gather around Michael. Michael senses something, but he is so overloaded with guilt, regret, sadness, and uncertainty that he allows his head to override the feelings in his gut. He looks directly at the car as Kione is pulling away.

Kione changes his tone again, this time sickly sweet, like the story tellers at the school assemblies. "Enough. Smile, we're going home now. Mommy is asleep, and soon you will be too."

The kids sit silently, tears falling down malnourished filthy cheeks. Jilly turns away empty of all hope or feeling.

30.

Michael is home, the full moon hanging in the sky behind some wispy clouds. His silhouette can be seen through the window in his office. Sleep will once again evade him as he tries to find something constructive to pass the time.

It's been eight weeks since he lost Merl. He sits at his computer looking at the moon out window. Surveying his surroundings thinking to himself 'This room is a mess. Papers, pictures, full ashtrays and empty bottles strewn around, I haven't slept for days and it shows. I am a disheveled mess, and the worst part is I really could give a flying fuck about it. If Merl was here she would kick my ass from here to Sunday, but that just doesn't matter anymore, does it?'

Dozer has taken to the furniture, as he stakes his spot on the corner sear of the couch he is watching Michaels every move.

"Don't look at me like that. I know I know, I promise, I will clean up a little bit. I just need to get some energy first, alright bud?" Dozer replies with a grunt and a loud fart.

Exasperated, the computer beckons. Michael turns to his newest yet most reliable friend, the glass of bourbon at his side. He types his lament to the others in the Elemental Prey Chat Room.

"Today was a bitch. I was informed of part of the estate I had no idea existed. I'm repulsed. I am now a rich man because of the loss of my family. The blood on my hands is turning into dollars in my wallet."

Elemental is glad to see Michael back. He lights a cigarette as his hands start typing the reply. He is in a dark home office with a flat screen computer flickering off of his face and body leaving him to look ethereal. The chat room is lively tonight. He takes a deep drag, cigarette smoke swirling in the light of the computer screen as he keys his reply.

"Do not torture yourself. You are a good man with good intentions. You did everything you could to save your family, but that was not what God had planned."

"And you know what God had planned?" Michael snapped back. Even through the screen his antipathy came through loud and clear.

"No, not personally, but I do know I started this group when I lost one of my own. No pain on earth can challenge that of a father when he loses his child. We were so close. Fate can be an evil whore."

Michael spots the vacation travel guide of Yosemite on Merl's night stand. The knot in his stomach tightens as acid crawls up his esophagus into the back of his throat. He finishes the bourbon and pour the second straight away. "I don't know what I would do if I hadn't found you. Sometimes this site and the friends I have made here are the only thing keeping me sane, or at least stopping me from going completely insane."

Elemental's words appear on computer screen. Michael reads the quietly, every once in a while looking at candid shots of Merleigh and the kids in photos all around Michael's office. Candid's and portraits, framed over the years as gifts or to celebrate special events, Christmas, delivery room shots. Then there is his favorite- Merl lying of the floor using Dozer as a pillow with Joey lying on his stomach looking at her bare nine month pregnant belly. He was talking to Jilly, already starting to bond with his little sister. Michael took that silent as a church mouse, without them realizing he was even in the room.

"I like to think that we can help. As men, it's not easy to talk about what we are going through. Man up, keep going, don't talk, stuff it down, suck it up, forget it, box it up and throw it away. Where do we go, who do we turn to when we are the ones people rely on?" Elemental seemed to know exactly what Michael was feeling,

"I have always been able to rely on myself. You tell me how I'm supposed to react." Michael pleaded. He was at the bitter end. "There must be some sort of rule of thumb about what to do, how to do it and when in these situations. There must be."

"You are supposed to be doing exactly what you're doing. Revenge my dear friend -- that is a dish best served..."

Michael thought that to be an odd response, but he know that is what would clear his soul. "Revenge, humph. How exactly do I go about that?" Michael takes a long swig of scotch, lights a cigarette with a prolonged exhale. "I don't even get to witness this fuck's sentencing. Part of the plea bargain."

"If you desire it to be, it will be. It is amazing how desire brings opportunities."

"What are you, fucking Kazoo from the Flintstones? You're missing the point. He's moved from predator to victim. He is turning into America's poster child for early intervention and Department of Youth and Family Services (DYFS) shortcomings. Kione doesn't look like a monster. He is articulate, charming, shy and self-deprecating. He is not what you would expect a torturous pedophile would be."

"I see. You said he is blaming his childhood? Psychopaths have a way of turning the facts around to portray themselves as the victims. The real victims of their lies and violence tend to get lost in the dust storm of deflection they create. Ah the media loves a protagonist, a phoenix from the ashes. We must not let them forget that you are the victim. We musn't allow his to forget what he has done."

Michael was feeling like he had a purpose. He was getting an adrenalin rush. "It's even harder when the twisted sexual predator that ruined your life is an Abercrombie & Fitch model prototype, no? I heard he is giving an exclusive to Fox, and that he has a book deal for his life story because he may end up in a mental half way house and not on death row."

"You have legal counsel? You must process a cease and desist order. Effective immediately!

"He can't make money from his crime, but he can profit off of a tortured, sad childhood full of psychological, emotional and physical abuse and neglect."

"Is that so? I wouldn't lose any more sleep my friend. The future has a way of working out."

31

Kione is speaking with the defense appointed expert therapist in San Quentin. They are in a calming room decorated in neutral colors with soft furniture and natural light from sky lights. He is sitting on an overstuffed chair with tears in his eyes sitting regaling his childhood. Flash backs of Kione as a child in the same tortuous situations as Joe and Jilly. In Kione's mind he and Joey and Jilly morph from one to another blurring reality and memories into his own version of acceptable behavior.

The therapist was an odd looking man. He is a cross between Ernest Hemingway and Jerry Garcia. He is a PH.D., graduate of Princeton, specializing in criminal psychiatric behavior for more the thirty years. He has worked all over the world with some of society's most heinous felons. In regard to the pits of hell that a human being can sink to there is really nothing he has not seen or heard. He is calloused yet professional.

Looking into Kione's eye, listening to him relive the torture-emotional, psychological, physical cruelty afflicted on him while expecting him to appear as a highly functional, over achieving perfect specimen of youth was mind boggling. The doctor actually had a twinge of empathy for the young man sitting before him. He would have no problem testifying that he was reachable and could be rehabilitated through strenuous therapy and deprogramming.

Kione answers all of the doctor's questions with such anguish and fear that the doctor himself felt protective and developed a personal vestment in his wellbeing.

32.

Michael continues, "He went after my kids because they were everything he wanted to be, they had everything he wanted to have."

"Retribution my friend, have you never heard of Newton's third law of physics? For every action there is an equal or greater reaction. Or, in other words- karma, the belief that every action one performs will bring upon oneself inevitable results, good or bad, either in this life or in the next. It's elemental to life my friend, just the basic principles.

33.

Inside the California Appellate Criminal Court Judge's Chambers of The Honorable Judge Humphry Channingsworth, who happens to be tasked with presiding over the Mitchell case. His robe hangs in corner on a brass coat rack. His chambers hold an inlaid mahogany desk, heavy and stately, walls lined with shelves atop of shelves of books, texts and tomes of laws from United States as well as abroad. The smell of lemon polish and worn leather bound books is an assault on the senses. The historical chamber omits an heir of patriotism and commands reverence.

The presiding Judge Channingsworth is in his mid-60s. He sits behind his highly polished desk. He by nature exudes confidence and arrogance. He knows that the case is a career maker or breaker. Being so close to retirement with an unblemished record there is nothing more he would rather see than to have this case disappear like a stain off of his tie while at the local cleaners.

He is in the middle of a one sided phone call, "Do you comprehend what you are asking of me? "

"This is one of the highest profile cases that have been before my court."

"I am responsible to public opinion as well as the letter of the law."

"I can appreciate the indignation and the bloodlust, but can you understand that the same demon is serving both the public and media feeding frenzy? "

"Yes but…" Standing starting to pace back and forth he is showing chinks in the professional armor. His skin grows warm, reddening at his collar. The vein in his left temple is beginning to throb.

"I suppose I can place a gag order due to the age of the victims, under a victim and family right to privacy act, strictly under the pretense that the victims were minors."

"Yes."

"You do understand that this will have a distinct affect my future if it gets out."

"No, I understand completely."

"Are you threatening me? You do realize who you are speaking to?"

"Do you know how far reaching my friends are?"

"No. No. No sir that is not a threat, merely a question."

"Yes, I am well aware of whom I am dealing with."

"I apologize I tend to get overly zealous."

"I truly appreciate your generosity and understanding."

34.

I never realized how much I would get from this personally, Elemental thought to himself as he surveyed the activity on his site. I realized there was an unanswered need, but for this amount of traffic, touching this many lives, well I must say I am quite satisfied with myself.

His fingers moved over the keyboard at lightning speed typing an e-mail as he hunched over the desk in his dark office, the only source of light coming from the screen of his computer. He clicks send and returns to the screen flickering with his chat room. He lights another cigarette from the glowing head of his current butt. He inhales sharply feeling the smoke fill up his lungs, enjoying a small rush from the oxygen deprivation and nicotine rushing into his system. He exhales watching the smoke swirling in the light of the computer screen.

He injects himself into the chat, "Good news my friends. I have a trip planned. I believe that some time away from all of the stress will help us regain control. I know it will be quite cathartic for everyone to get to know each other on a personal level and help each other to achieve our goals. The trip will be for ten days. If this is something you may be interested in, please let me know as soon as possible. Below is the link to sign up. Space is limited, so please do not delay."

35.

A large military cargo plane lands and pulls into a hanger. The prisoners are being moved like animals to slaughter one at a time. Hooded and chained by feet and hands. Armed guards are moving each prisoner from point A to point B, pistol whipping them if they make a sound.

A man with a Dragunov sniper rifle makes a sharp turn and beats one of the dozen prisoners in the kidneys with the butt of his rifle for coughing. In a low, almost inaudible whisper with a strong Guyanese accent he advises the prisoner "Don't make me tell you one more time, mother fucker. I would love nothing more than to skin you alive so you are aware just what we are capable of. I've got my eye on you son."

Inside a bunker housing the inmates, mosquitoes and bugs are crawl up their naked skin, flying into their mouths if they try to breathe the heavy humid air with their mouths open. The oppressive heat creates a sheen of sweat and dirt on their skin. They are placed in a completely blacked out, soundproof bunker built under the lodge.   It is devoid of any stimulation designed specifically to totally obstruct the five senses.

The prisoners slowly start their descent into a mental hell unaware that there are others suffering the same anguish simultaneously. The inmate taken from New Orleans feels his lips cracking from dehydration. He leans against the wall and feels a liquid seeping out of the concrete. He places his lips against the wall allowing the dripping water to collect on the tip of his tongue. His stomach aches from hunger, he grabs a large beetle as it runs up his leg and chews down of it, the hunger overpowering the urge to vomit from the crunch and ooze in his mouth.

He starts to pray, "Our father, who art in heaven..."

A masked guard appears as soon as the prisoner opens his mouth and slips a rope around his neck. The guard drags him with the rope, smacking him against boulders and rock walls while choking him. His skin is being scraped from his body is agonizing sue to the hyper state of his senses from being deprive for so long.

Days have passed.   Music is being used to set to "fire" short bursts of acoustic energy, causing the prisoners to feel spatial disorientation they are deprived of all other sights, smells or sounds. No food or clean water yet.

The convict from New York starts rocking back and forth, hugging himself. Pleading, "Dear God. Please... No. I beg... Please... no no no..."

36.

The lodge is coming along much better than I had anticipated though elemental as he surveyed the property and the work that had been accomplished since the most recent visit to the island. He was proud of the exquisite craftsmanship of the main cabin made from local wood. The lead windows, the verandas that extended from each level offering breathtaking views of the island. From this lodge, one could view three hundred and sixty degrees of the island, land and sea from every vantage point. He was pleased and his men would see it when they received their bonuses.

He entered the main foyer and took an elevator to the send floor where the technical command center was staged. The room held multiple flat screens that were strategically linked with various cameras hidden throughout. There was not an inch of space on this island that he would not observe with a swipe of his finger. All elements were under his control. Looking at a state of the art security camera system on a screen divided into six each quadrants he eyed each prisoner. He felt a perverse gratification watching the prisoners living the way they deserved.

He smirks snidely as he speaks to himself. "I do enjoy it when the tables are turned and the predator becomes the prey."

Onscreen, one of the L.A. prisoners grunts, vomits, moans.

37.

Inside the bunker a personal hell is being created for each prisoner, using various techniques of torture. After days of food and water and sleep deprivation, they are given a meal. The meal is laced with psychotropic drugs. The prisoners scarf down the sustenance despite the intestinal pain from lack of food. Their bellies have shrunken down and now the rapid expansion is excruciating, yet they eat because they have no idea when they will be given their next meal.

The drugs are starting to kick in. The men who have attempted to retain what little control of the minds and surrounding that they could muster are losing to the pharmaceuticals coursing through their veins and taking over their minds.

Thrash metal is being blared into the bunker containing the inmates. The so called meals are finished and it is time to start the rotations. New York is placed into a cold box, made to induce hypothermia and frost bite by standing on blocks of ice in bare feet for hours until the cold feels like fire and his toes start to turn brown. L.A. prisoner is having electrodes attached to his testicles while being water boarded. Meanwhile the New Orleans inmate is hanging from his wrists in a coffin style cell the walls so close that the slightest movement scrapes his skin against the jagged rocks that are closing in on him.

Kione is there, amongst the vermin. He is alone with a gag ball in his mouth, sitting in a water tank that is slowly rising to his nose.

38.

The crescent moon rising red in the east while the sun making its final decent from in the sky. This has always been Michael's favorite part of the day, the time for life to switch gears and return from the stress of the day to life's natural rhythms. Tonight Michael is sitting on his back steps smoking a cigarette. The usual position, drink in hand. Looking disheveled, his hair in need of a cut and his beard starting to grow in. He is a chain smoker, running at about two and a half packs a day, using the beer bottle as an ashtray. Dozer, his constant companion is lying at his feet, raised his head, thumping his tail as Danny's truck appeared in the driveway.

Danny walks into the back yard following a cloud of smoke. "Hey, you are one hard guy to get a hold of. Where the hell have you been?" Danny walks up and mushes Dozers droopy jowls in between his hands and gives him a big kiss on the top of his head, turning to Michael he messed his brothers hair. This move was usually a declaration of war tonight Michael barely notices the show of affection.

"I have been right here. It's not like I have had a full social calendar lately."

"Come on, why don't we go inside." Danny leans over to grab hold of Michael and inhales sharply.

"I'll order a Chinese, Dim Sum sounds divine." As Michael walks by Danny scowls at the stench oh body odor his brother is emitting. "Damn, shower lately? God damn you smell like something the cat dragged in and threw back up. WTF dude, did they turn your water off or something?"

"I'm fine. You didn't need to come. I showered just…" He couldn't remember. "I don't need anything. Thanks for stopping, I'll call you"

Danny leans over. Michael sways as he knocks over beer bottles lined up on the steps. "OK, I get that you are in a weird place, but Mer would be doing flips in her grave if she thought her house was turning into Trailer Park Place. Dude, do you not see what a hole this place is turning into? Hell, I am worried about Dozer. Do not make me call one of those cable shows on you man, you know I will."

Michael becomes slightly combative. "You leave my only friend out of this. He's the only family I have."

Danny tries to keep the mood light. "Thanks I think. Can't wait to get the DNA results off of that, but where does that leave me?" He winces dramatically for effect. "Yo, shower time, man. You go hit it while I order up the pizza. And BTW we ARE going to clean up before the Niners game. Health Dept. ordered it."

Michael tries to act sober, fails. "K, I know man. I love you, bro. I really love you, bro. Dozer loves you, bro."

The two go inside the house, Michael hanging on Danny's shoulder. The house is in worse shape since Danny's last visit. Garbage and bottles are strewn around the house full ashtrays overflowing. The leftover take out containers are crusty and sticking to the counter. The aroma of riding behind a garbage truck on a summer day is making Danny's eyes water.

Something major has to be done, Danny thought, there is no way I can let my brother live this way. I have to figure out what and I gotta figure it out fast.

39.

Eric was sitting at his desk lost deep somewhere inside himself. His biggest client had unreal expectations and wanted everything done yesterday. Fortunately his client was ex CIA, so anything he wanted he has the resources to fulfill. Even the most extravagant requests were optioned and exacted. The mobile phone rang, startling him. Looking at his watch he answers knowing who's on the line. "Michael."

"Hey bro, sorry I haven't gotten back to you."

"I was getting ready to call the cops and have 'em check on you my man. Where've you been?" Eric was aggravated as he raked his perfectly manicured hands through his thick styled hair.

"Busy doing some thinking."

Eric realized the irony in that statement as he played with the onyx pinky ring.

"Danny is here, he said the same thing to me. Guess I have been incognito for a while, huh?"

"You can't keep doing this to us. Danny called me asking if I'd seen you. We don't need this shit from you."

"I think I need to get my head together. I have this chance to go on a trip though that website you gave me."

"Really? Go on." Eric tried to ignore the ominous feeling he was getting in the pit of his stomach. He also realized that his nervous habit of spinning the ring was starting to cause callouses and that meant he was under too much stress.

Michael was seated on the foot of his bed, still wet from the shower. The droplets being absorbed into the silk comforter were making an odd amoeba shape. He was slowly sobering up and clearing his head. The discomfort of the wet bed suddenly dawned on him as he shifted to another seat.

He continued on with the framework of the trip. This is the first thing he has had to look forward to in years, and it seems to be the answer to is prayers. "The program is called Elemental Journey. Anyway, it's a ten day retreat that is supposed to help clear out the source of negativity from my life. You know the guy who runs the site you hooked me up with? Anyway, his nom de plume is 'Elemental' hence the name Elemental Journey."

Without taking a breath since he started reciting his plans to him Mike enthusiastically carried on. Eric could sense the anticipation of a renaissance in Mike's tone of voice. "He said it's just what I need, what we need. I am not sure if this guy is an actual therapist, but he seems to be helping me. HE seems pretty legit."

Danny is moving around in the background trying not to eavesdrop overtly yet hanging on every word of the one sided conversation.   He looks at his brother with curiosity and concern, something is not setting right. He ignores his premonitions and chalks them up to being overprotective.

Privacy is not something that should be abused, so Danny moves to setting up the kitchen for dinner and giving dozer fresh water and a new bowl of food.

40.

Back in the bedroom, Michael is now on speaker as he towels off the remaining moisture, adding deodorant and aftershave.

"Ok, tell me more." Eric's voice suddenly on loud speaker startling Mike with the volume of the disembodied voice.

Danny looks over his shoulder, for a moment he could have sworn that Eric was in the other room.

Grabbing his washed out black denim jeans, his grey button down knit shirt and his favorite black snakeskin belt, he thought to himself this feels good. I feel pretty good. Grabbing the phone and placing it on the edge of the dresser he decides to leave the volume at ten while carrying on the conversation.

"Yeah, so check it out. Ten days in the tropics of Guyana- supposedly a state of the art retreat."

"Well, it sounds like you have your mind already made."

"I dunno. I want to, but it seems a little weird."

"Alright, I'll check it out. Make sure it's legit."

"If you would that would be stellar. I really don't trust my judgment at the moment."

Danny hears the last snippet and can't hold back from adding his two cents. Yelling at the top of his lungs, "None of us do."

Michael is slightly unenthused and ignores the peanut gallery remarks. Not helping is the laugh hidden by a fake cough coming from the other end of the phone. "On second thought, I think I may just stay home. It's a long way away. It is a pricey trip and besides what about Dozer? I can't just leave him. He needs me."

Eric is exasperated and almost sea sick from the ups and downs of this conversation. He walks over and leans against the glass panel windows. The feel of the coolness from the glass against his forehead, the slight vertigo of the bay and surrounding area looking so small from way up here, something about the feeling he may fall through any moment gives him a rush of adrenaline and brings him back to center. He inhales sharply and responds to his friend in earnest "I know you'll be worried about that drooling snoring farting mass of mess but don't. I can take him. Hell he can even come to the office with me. Between Danny and me, he'll be livin' la Vida petro!

Mike saunters into the kitchen looking at the mastiff lying at his feet, snoring. "Really, you'd do that for me?" He is so in love with that dog. Dozer has been his thread holding him from going over the edge. "Thanks man. He's the one thing left that I would give my life for."

"You know we've got your back. You do realize that if I spend any more time on the phone with you it's going to cost you about ten dollars a minute and that is the family plan."

"Family? What about I do what I do for love?"

"Pro bono? Bullshit. I am working late -- beers at the pub, at eight?

"I'm in no shape. How about you come over here hang with da boys. Danny is here already and you can pick up dinner on the way. I will call it in. Does Greek make your heart skip a beat?"

"K. I could use some Dozer drool. Gyro's always seem to do it for him."

"Cool, we'll see you in a few. Oh, thanks…"

"Yeah, see you in a few." Eric hung up the phone cutting Mike off midstream.

41.

He had much to do, no time to do it in and all of it coming to a head at one time.

Danny grabbed the last antibacterial wipe and shined the counter. The smell of chemicals and lemon finally overthrew the stale tobacco and beer. Mr. Clean I am not Danny thought to himself, but I am winning the war on gunk and grime. Wow, too much TV and not enough social life. Gotta get out more. Note to self… as fast as yesterday.

Mike was watching Danny and could tell that he was having one of his internal arguments. He always had a face that couldn't hide a thing. It might as well have been written across his forehead since he was three. No matter where or when, a poke face was something he was born without.

"Danny boy, you alright there?"

Danny just looked at him, shook his head scrubbing away.

"Eric is coming over, Greek tonight. He said you and he would take over for me with Dozer. Is that cool with you"

Danny smiled, "I if take him, you may never get him back." He moved away from his chores and snuggled up to the imposing mass of spit and fur on the floor. Dozer took his oversized paw and cradled Danny as if he were a child. Danny lit up like a boy on Christmas morning. Dozer nuzzled into his neck and licked his face. Mike watched knowing that they needed each other too.

42.

Eric was processing the conversation that he had just had. Details, some were adding up, some needed a fresh pair of eyes on them. Turning the onyx ring round and round his finger as he sat pondering the situation he absently watched the sun set. As if suddenly aware of the time, he turned quickly in his leather chair back to his desk.

He intercom his secretary, voice tight, tone sharp and threatening, "I have a conference call. Hold all my calls. Do not disturb me until I give you notice, is that clear?" There was not and immediate response. "I asked is that clear?"

"Yes sir. Crystal."

Picking up phone, he waits a few moments. All of a sudden his mouth is dry cotton formed on his tongue and in the back of his throat. He notices his palms are clammy yet he is chilled to the bone as if the room temperature has dropped ten degrees. He steadies himself with a shot of scotch. His usual remedy for the jitters, yet this not a normal case of nerves. His remedy was making him feel bilious, waves of nausea washed over him.

Compose yourself man! This is what you do, this is who you are. Be damned if you let something like this get the better of you! He was his own best advocate, yet his internal pep talk seemed to incongruous this time.

"Yes. Very well thank you." He proceeded with the one sided conversation.

He felt as if he were a child in the principal's office again.

"The meetings have gone as planned and the assets are in escrow, just as we discussed." Claustrophobia was never an ailment of his, yet the symptoms seemed to be congealing second by second. The walls felt closer than they ever had before.

"No problems. The transitional period should be approximately two weeks." Each word was harder to form, maybe it was vertigo. He felt sweat seeping through his flawlessly starched Brooks Brothers pinstripe dress shirt.

"No, I don't see foreseeable issues." Did his voice just crack? Was he starting to hear things?

"Thank you." Time was standing still, than seconds appeared to become hours as if he had entered a different dimension.

"You have been more than generous during our negotiations." He loosened his tie. Sipped upon his scotch feeling his jaw muscles clench so tightly that he had to force them to move when he spoke. They ached with tension.

"The records of accounting are available to you through our secure server. Yes. I believe we are working under budget. We have specialists who are trained to specifically handle these situations working very hard." This can't be happening. He is too good for this. The best there is, yet he wants so badly to please that he is paralyzed.

"No. No sir. I don't foresee any surprises." What has him so worried? He has all of the answers, and they are the right answers. The secret to his success has always been playing three moves ahead of his clients and five moves ahead of the opposition. His head was throbbing. He clasped onto the side arm of the chair for stability.

"Thank you. I agree we have a very amicable working relationship. Why was this happening? He gulped air, trying to prevent a full blown panic attack. "Yes, I realize the ramifications if" Now he couldn't get a full sentence out.

"No sir, I would never" This is not good, he had to regain control of the situation. "Yes sir. I too look forward to a long relationship."

When the conversation had ended, Eric felt as if he had aged a decade. He never had a propensity to please others unless doing so had benefitted him directly yet he had an unnatural need not only to please but to gain the respect and possible adulations from this man.

He got up and tried to shake off the feeling of doubt creeping into his psyche. Mindlessly turning his ring with his thumb, he paced for a moment following the pattern on the marble floor. The matters with Mike must be wearing my skin thin. Let me get started on his trip, as soon as I can get him settled there is a definitive possibility that my edges will again sharpen. Focus damn it, focus!

43.

Somewhere off the coast of Guyana another day is about to start. The sun rises as the steam from the jungle takes a choke hold over the camp. Men are putting in hours of manual labor. Cutting through the thick foliage, cutting passages with machetes to maneuver equipment through the dense flora and digging trenches, laying pipes and creating a human habitat where only a few weeks ago there was none.

Like ants marching in a colony, the men work tirelessly barely acknowledging each other, all with one main objective. If all goes as planned, they will be rewarded for their efficiency as well as for their confidentiality. The men were all chosen with careful consideration being given not only to their specialty and their craftsmanship, but to their living conditions and their place on the social continuum. The bulk of the laborers were stoic, by choice or by chance life had made them hard and distrusting of others. Each was excellent at observing the rules, and had a proclivity for executing orders meticulously without questioning authority or the reasoning behind the task.

As the worked hour upon hour the progress was visible. There were over 500 men working on the project, yet none of them except a select few knew what it was they were doing. Even the foremen on the job only had access to their specific plans which encompassed only a module of the entire encampment. The lay out was a labyrinth, each portion only accessible through another, and even then each section was out of the line of site of the prior. An architect may say it is the design of a madman. Taking inspiration from the Winchester Mystery House near his home in California, he decided that a 6 level encampment, with 3 of those levels being subterranean would suit his needs perfectly. With corridors and staircases that appeared to lead to nowhere. Even in the main facility, the guest rooms and the public areas held crevices, and secret stairways, rooms that one could enter yet not exit from unless they knew the lever or key or code of lifter books, dialed numbers or spoken words. Unlike the spirit house he adored, nothing here was left to chance. Every nail, every board, every electronic device played a crucial role in the future success of this encampment.

Should the inaugural experiment go off as planned, he foresaw a great destiny, one that may change the world once his systems were proven and gained acceptance. The excitement started to build as he watched his dreams take shape.

44.

The prisoners being rotated from one torture to the next while the guard is holding his semi-automatic to the nape of the man's neck while texting his progress on his iPhone with the opposite hand attaching a picture of the scene before him.

From the far away a muffled cry escapes from a rat pit as another prisoner feels the hungry rodents start to feed on his salty sweat sheened flesh. "Please just let me die. Please, just let me die. Dear God help me. Help me…NOOOO!"

A guard overhears the man's pleas, laughs to himself as if this entity would be able to help him. The guard actually believes it was the man's sins that have him here in the first place and it is that God who is making him pay for his turpitudes on this earth instead of in the afterlife. Something about that scenario makes the guard feel righteous indignation and a perverse sense of enjoyment.

45.

As the darkness cloaked his home, his heart, sitting at his computer Michael typed fiercely at moments then sat staring while the minutes developed into hours. Danny on the couch behind him playing with the dog, Eric sipped his drink leaning against the desk reaching into the top draw removing the remote to turn on the Niner's game.

"All I have to do is sign up. Everything is included." He was excited for the first time in two years. "They will send a car to pick me up, travel there, food, booze. Everything! Can you believe it?"

"I haven't had a chance to check it out for you yet." Eric mumbled not wanting to change the momentum of the room.

"Sounds like exactly what the doctor ordered to help me get my shit together." Michael was lying off the booze- for the most part and more importantly showering consistently for the past few days, on and off. He even went so far as to take Dozer to the vet for his shots without anyone having to nag him. Thanks to his upcoming retreat.

"Yeah, exactly where are you going? I mean what if this is some big scam? It's all kind of secretive. You know, I don't want you getting kidnapped by some pirates or drug cartel there bro." Danny lit his cigarette, emptying the overflowing ashtray. He looked over his shoulder, cigarette clenched in his teeth opening a window. The smell was potent so he grabbed and sprayed Febreeze into the air, forming an indoor lavender scented smog cloud of tobacco and chemicals. "God

Damn bro, it smells like an ashtray and gym bag in here. I had to beg you to shower. Now you're telling me you're ready to get away on your own when you still can't manage to empty a fuckin ashtray? Did you even consider who is going to take care of Dozer?

Danny plays tug-of-war with the now awake dog. Thank God he can hide behind the game hoping the sting of his comment flew over his brother's head.

"I got it all taking care of. I said you and I would take him. I was hoping you wouldn't pass up a chance to pick up some ladies while bonding with this lug." Eric was always the diplomat. Danny knew him like family but Eric was Michael's go to guy. There was something about him Danny never could quite put his finger on it. Yet, whenever he was around Eric for a prolonged time he got this feeling in the pit of his stomach that something in the world was just a hair off course.

By the way, bro, you'll be happy to know that while I'm away I am getting the place painted and new rugs. Need a new start. Obviously..." He opens his arms, turns around, indicating the mess all around him. "The first step should be taken with other guys like me. We are all really different, granted, but we're all coming from the same place."

"I hear ya. But I still feel like you are going to be drinking Kool-Aid and waiting for UFO's. If they suggest a certain designer sneaker promise me you'll get the fuck out!"

"You are one cold son of a bitch." Eric shot at Danny. "You shoulda been the lawyer."

Danny grins, "No thank you very much, one of you is plenty."

Michael starts to pace. He pours bourbon, mulling over what his brother just said. "Just shut up and listen for once. There's this guys who is a businessman in New Orleans. This poor son of a bitch almost loses it all during Katrina. His wife and daughter leave to go to grab dinner and a movie and are never heard from again."

"Mike don't, I can't!" For the first time even the Great Danny didn't want the particulars of these sad minuets.

"Some mother fucker carjacks them and keep them for days to torture. And after they're dead, keeps them as his family! What the fuck?" Mike proceeded as if he was talking to himself, dissecting the human psyche behind violent criminals, as if he was part profiler part super hero.

"That's some sick shit. But that's life, bro. Ya hear it on the news, read it in the paper, see it online. It is what it is. Move on, you can't own every victim, every crime as if it is a personal assault on you. Move past it, maybe you can even try isolating yourself from it for a while until your skin gets thicker and you are strong again?" Danny was once again grasping at straws. He was losing his edge trying to keep hold of the brother he adored.

"Danny…." He exhaled through his nose, calculating his next sentence very carefully. "Do you really need to? Lighten the fuck up man." A reality check was just as god as a text book over the head on occasion.

Danny went to Dozer and snuggling with him on the couch. Danny is getting agitated and trying to keep his cool, redirecting his attention to the mutt was soothing momentarily. 'As long as people walk this earth there will be some evil bastards out there. It's the way man is wired. Nothing we can do about it except move on."

"You just don't get it do you? These are the extremes and they are becoming the norm! Wake the fuck up there little bro, we need to do something about this and damn soon before we become like some weird ass sci-fi movie where we are all armored and armed to the teeth all the time. We are desensitized and you're proof of it! Just, just listen," Michael was walking in circles at warp speed, moving his hands in big sweeping gestures, over compensating and over acting to get his point across. "There's the guy from LA. His daughter and her best friend took their dog for a hike on the trails in the mountains behind his house. A Mexican drug cartel grabbed them. Picture it guys, the dog comes back home beat to shit and the girls were gone." His skin was glistening from a forming sheen of sweat, his jugular vein starting to pulse visible to the naked eye as he continues ranting. "These sons of bitches forced these girls to work in a bordello as sex slaves right here in L.A. Right here in our back yards! Dontcha see? Don't you get it?!?"

"Do you really think it's a good idea to be submerged in this?" Danny was throwing Michael a life line hoping he would grab on and not let go.

"Danny, there's a name for it. Submersion therapy, if he's gonna move past it he has to move through it." Eric always with the level head, always with the right answers to all the hard questions. Something about this wasn't sitting right with Danny and he wasn't ready to let it go.

46.

"In ten full days we will combine the healing power of nature, sportsmanship and camaraderie into a life altering experience." The father from LA reads the brochure.

Two preteen girls being dressed like prostitutes. One in spandex purple hot pants with cut outs up on side and down the other while the other girl is wearing a baby doll dress that barely covers the cheeks of her ass.

They receive lecherous looks from the Mexican gang members, the men suck air through their teeth yelling at them and pawing them like they were meat.

They are passed from man to man much like a lit joint. They see each other. They try to speak, to scream for help when they hear a radio of a cop outside their door. The men guarding the room will have none of that. They take her to the tunnel that is used to mule cocaine from Tijuana under the city streets to the distribution centers. Under the ground, a bare light bulb hangs off a wire. The air is stagnant and reeks of urine. The young child is not sure what is happening or where she is going, this is the first time she has been completely separated from her best friend. Three more men appear seemingly out of nowhere.

One man has the machete licking the blade makes his tongue bleed. This incites him. He looks at the other two men, who grab her arms while knocking her legs out from under her. They pin her to the ground on her stomach. The larger of the two starts to rape her from behind. She cries out, turning her head, as the smaller man places his hand on her head, his palm over her ear pushing her cheek into the sand and grit floor. She tries to bite him, and with that the man with the machete grabs her tongue and yanks it out as far as he possibly can. She is screaming. She feels her tongue as it is being ripped from its root. She gags while she cries out in pain as her mouth fills with blood. It feels cavernous.

She realizes what they have just done to her. She starts to puke from the blood flowing down her throat and from the realization that she no longer possesses a tongue. She eyes those men through hot stinging tears as they hold the pink muscle up in from of her. The machete wielder stabs it in the center and places it on his chain next to the medal of the virgin mother.

Meanwhile in the bordello, which is located in the back of an illegal cantina, lean-to's and rooms made from clap board stuffed with old mattresses packed into back allies awaiting the next client are filled with illegal sex workers, a majority of them trafficked into the country after being kidnapped from their homes in Mexico. There are the few Americans who ended up here by owing their dealers or by seeing or being someplace the cartel deemed inappropriate.

A black van pulls up and the door flings open. The girl in the baby doll dress is crying. She is now 6 months pregnant. The door slam shut. She is tied down and gagged while a back alley abortionist scraped the unborn child from her womb. The van has blood all over the walls and floor. The girl is wreathing in pain- the blood is rushing out of her pooling between her legs. Her eyes roll into the back of her head. She is unconscious. Her labored breathing ceases. As the van pulls away a bag is dumped out of the rear doors. The bag remains there for four days, in the heat amongst the rats and roaches until the smell becomes insuperable and a neighbor calls the board of health. The police are alerted upon the gruesome discovery of the body and the bordello.

The police round the girls, finding that there was an Amber Alert out for the two teens. Best friends. Now one is dead and one is mute from the torcher bored upon her. She writes her name and asks for her father.

The police contact him at one. The L.A. Man is screaming in his head, his stomach in knots, his heart physically hurting from the story that the detectives are relating to him of his daughters predicament. Picturing his daughter mouth being held open and a shadow shot of a man swinging a machete. Ripped bloody white sheet stained with bodily fluids being used as a gag and to stop the bleeding. The man puts his hands to his temples as if his head is about to explode. The detectives are giving him advice how to handle his daughter after the ordeal she has been through. They are giving him cards of social service workers, psychiatrists, and medical and legal representation. After all, his daughter was a sex worker and the DA may be filing charges.

47.

Michael ignored Danny and Eric and went on. "The cops found the girls because the best friend died during a late term abortion and was thrown into the trash. This guy's twelve year-old daughter was found in a back room, dressed like a whore, chained to a bed with her tongue cut out."

"I really don't need the gory details. Mike, neither do you. Stop already. Don't you have enough on your own plate then to start eating off of someone else's dirty dish? I don't think I can handle hearing any more tonight."

"Yeah, yeah ya can. You need to know why you will never be part of this club. God willing and why it is so imperative that I join."

"I hear ya Mike. We both do. We are behind you one hundred percent. Danny and I both want nothing more than to see you healed and hopefully helping others will be the conduit that you need to get you to the other side. Don't you agree Danny?" Eric looked over to Danny for support with a knowing glance that said cut him off at the pass and move quick.

"Danny, you needed to know why I can't talk to people who can't deal with the dirty details. You're one of them. It makes your clean, pristine word dirty at the edges and you want to run, lock your doors and play Sinatra. Great, have at it, but you can't go through this and not be fucked up."

Eric rolls up his sleeves and grabs another slice of cold pizza. He pointed to the Bourbon and his empty glasses with bottle in hand. "Another round boys?"

Danny nods passes him his glass. Exasperated, defensive and ready to remove his gloves and let Mike take the win this round he pleads, "I got it, but you need real help man. Not some fucking free website that is going to drag your sorry ass into the jungles in the middle of East Bumblefuck."

48.

The man from New York read the brochure. "Day two, meet and greet. Put a face to the name and get an introduction to the rules and regulations of the games."

He remembers all too well his little girl crying in a room with no windows. The decorations a sick fantasy world of a bastardized fairytale land slash S&M dungeon. The room had a white canopy bed, soft lilac walls with castles painted on them. Chains and various torture devices mixed with teddy bears and dollies shelved and bed side tables. Some had their eyes removed other were I various stages of torture, mutilation and unease. A man with thinning greasy brown hair, thick glasses had sweat dripping down his overgrown sweep over. He licks his lips in anticipation while reading a computer screen. He has a world of perversion giving their input as to what fait this little angel should befall that evening. He regaled the little girl with stories of what "sickprick33" wants him to do to her like a father telling her a bed time story.

Her father helpless, glued to the monitor knowing he may be just yards or miles away from his girl. His eyes are tight on computer screen. He is trying to will his daughter free. Amplified by terror and shame he could hear his little girl's bloodcurdling scream and it burned into his memory as if he were being branded by a hot iron. It was inhuman the hundreds of comments suggesting various tortures and abuse being flashed onto the screen from anonymous screen names from around the globe.

"Yeah" Nodding in recollection, sheepishly slouching from guilt, Danny remembers that story. The girl had the hearts of America, the heart of the world.

"That was all over the news. I can't believe that guy didn't go totally insane" Eric was talking about her father.

"Remember her Danny? The world watched as she was tortured, raped and mutilated. It was on every news channel. Posted to Deep Web links, the new world version of dark alleys where illicit minds go to find whatever vice, perversion, sin, or crime against humanity you can imagine is available, anonymously and with a stroke of a key. Name it, and some sadistic mother had it as a favorite."

"People are fascinated by the macabre. To them, it wasn't real, ya know? Then there were the rest of us who didn't know what to do, so we watched and waited." Danny was never so thankful for an ice filled beverage in his life as he inhaled the sweet woody scent of the bourbon and took a long slow draw from his glass. His knuckles were white from holding on to the beverage for dear life, a slight change in pressure and the glass would have imploded pushing shards through his skin leaving his hand as bloody and raw as his nerves.

"The FBI, Interpol, techs and geeks at MIT, Apple and Microsoft- the best technology geniuses in the world at their disposal and yet nobody could figure out where the hell this guy was keeping her. He had signals being pinged all over the universe." Michael orated this as if he were speaking to diplomats at the UN, looking into a crowd of faceless people looking at no one at all."

49.

Danny turned around to check the score on the TV, tuning his brother out just for a reprieve. For Danny there was a security to knowing that life was going on as usual outside the crazy in these walls. He found solace in the sounds of the announcer's voices deciphering their little arguments over stats and boundaries. He got up and left Eric with Michael. Walking into the dark bathroom he left the lights off. He didn't need to look at his reflection and have it parrot back to him what he already knew. He was overwhelmed. Splashing some cool water over his face, running his hands through his hair to dry them off was the interruption he needed to clear his head and return to his post as faithful comrade and confessor. When he returned to the room Dozer intentionally scooted his ever so large body into a small ball making room for his favorite uncle. "I can't look at that anymore. This shit makes my stomach turn. Why do you need anyone else's drama? Do you not have enough of your own?"

Michael was begging for empathy. "The father just sat at his computer, every day, helpless. He sat, looking for a sign, a hint, anything to take him to his little girl." He walked over and kneeled next to his brother, putting his hand on Danny's arm. "They finally found this twisted bastard because his neighbor was stealing his cable. The cable guy saw the images while performing a line test cutting off his neighbor's access."

"As a lawyer who is versed in subversion and twisting facts to make a point may I ask on behalf of the somewhat sane 'How the hell can someone do that?' It's so cruel and sick and twisted on so many levels. Who even thinks of this shit?"

"See, you'll just never understand, man, you guys 'ill just never get it."

Danny stands up and squares off, eye to eye with his brother. "How dare you, you mother fucker. I was here, or don't you remember? You made them my family too! Get off of your solo fucking high horse and get a grip."

"Calm down, both of you" Eric pleaded as he took the familiar spot between them, a hand on each chest. "Back the truck up."

Danny was tenacious the proverbial last straw had just been planted. "You sorry ass son of a bitch I am so sick and fuckin tired of the Michael pity party. We were all here Mike. I walked the park, I handed out flyers, was here when you found Merl. What the fuck don't I get? I think are so fucking out of touch with reality that if it came and bit you in the left nut the right one wouldn't even notice!"

With such a candid portrait painted Mike and Eric both looked stunned momentarily as the covered their zippers subconsciously. With that the tension subsided and all three started to laugh. Not any laugh but a cleansing belly laugh that had been a long missing element and now as welcomed to return.

Michael sat down to catch his breath and turned sheepishly to his brother, "Your right, I know."

"You are such a selfish, ungrateful fuck." With that Danny wrapped his arm around Mike's neck putting him in a head lock while giving him the worst noogie he could muster since he was in eighth grade. Mike squirmed and yelled, hooped and hollered under Danny's tight grip. His head felt like it was on fire and that Danny was simultaneously yanking his hair out from the roots and giving him rug burn!

Mike hoped the commotion would be cut short when Dozer realized what was happening. No such luck, Dozer just lay there as Eric rubbed his ears and the two eyed the bravado of the brothers auspiciously.

"Okay, Okay, Danny, chill the fuck out." Eric felt that things may be going from playful too dangerous in a flash. He thought right, and in the nick of time. He could see it in Mike's red face and the clenched jaw of Danny the oppressor.

Danny shook Mikes hand then gave him one of his signature bear hugs, mea culpa style. Mike could never stay mad at Danny, vice versa. "Mike I just don't know if this is a good idea, bro. I'm all you got to protect you. How am I gonna do that from thousands of miles away?

I don't know where you're going, who you're going with and where to go if you need me."

"Does this mean you two kissed and make up?"

The brother's responded in unison to Eric's snarky comment, "Bite me."

"I think you need to move forward. I hope you're making the right decision bro. If this is what you really need to do, I got your back. Hanging out in person with a bunch of people who are stuck in this abyss of revenge? I gotta tell you it just doesn't feel good to me one bit."

"No man, that's not what it's like. Trust me will ya?"

"But why in the middle of nowhere?"

"The location is to stave off the media. 100% complete anonymity and privacy.

"Reliving and rehashing this sick shit again and again and again? It's sadistic, bro."

"I know you're uncomfortable Danny, but we need to back him up."

"Eric, what the fuck do you think I've been doing?

"Come around man. You have my word, he'll be safe."

"Fuck you both." Michael seethed, tired of being treated like a child. "I need to do this to move on. I need to do this to get that fucking monkey off of my back. Eric, I don't need you permission. I am going, and whatever the two of you agree to or not is none of my concern. You can' think what you want, just promise me when get home Dozer will be the same lump of lard as when I left."

50

"Okay, what the hell? You are one loose fucking cannon man. Drop it down a notch." Eric was the only one that could get away with that, ever.

"Yeah… I feel responsible for the death of my kids, and especially the death of Merl. I gotta do this. It's just something that is out of my hands. It's beyond my control."

"Do what you have to do. Whatever you decide, we got you covered with the house, with Dozer. I'll have my staff get all of the finances in order. Go and do what you feel you need to do. Promise us one thing, that when you get back you will hop back on the fucking horse and start living life again. Closure, I get it, Danny gets it, but you have to get it too. Enough of the bullshit, agreed?"

"Eric, don't speak for me." Staring at Michael standing with his arms crossed in front of him very defensive. "Fine- I am happy that you found people who get you."

"Really, are you?"

"I am so happy that this is what you think you need. I am gonna tell you this, man, you should be getting help from a professional." Danny turns his attention back to Eric, "Not some cyber-fuckin-monkey BS that is going to tell you whatcha wanna hear and milk you out of thousands of dollars in some foreign fuckin country. HELLO?!?!? JONESTOWN anyone?!?"

"Danny, I would never do anything to hurt either of you. I have clients who have gone down a similar route. It is the newest thing and it helped them immensely. I will personally guarantee that your brother will come to no bodily harm during this quest."

"Dude this is the shit movies are made out of. Just because Eric gives it the Pope's blessing doesn't make it gospel. I got a bad feeling about this. Please do me a favor and reconsider. Maybe go next month or the month after that. Back burner it for a while, that's all."

"Standing right here. Hello?!?" Eric had placed himself in between Danny and Michael again waving his hand in Danny's face while protecting his best friend from his brother's attacks.

"Maybe, just maybe if people would stop treating me like I am an invalid. Maybe, if people would just leave me the fuck alone. Maybe, just maybe I could start to live my life again. I do not need kid gloves, or a straightjacket, and I am not suicidal."

"Could've fooled us." Danny gestured, sweeping the room that looked like it belonged on an episode of hoarders.

"You're just wound tight right now. We are all running a few cylinders high. Let's all take a breather and just let it be for a bit. We can revisit this at any time."

"No Eric, I need to get away. I need to breathe again. Just give me this one than I promise, if I need it, I'll go to as many headshrinkers as you can find in the South Bay. Until then just back off, 'k?"

51.

The men from are sitting at their computers, each reading a portion of the trip itinerary.

Michael reads the line written under a beautiful photo hunting lodge nestles in rainforest foliage. "Ten days all-inclusive in a lush tropical setting."

New Orleans Man continues the paragraph half way across the country, his lips move but the sound of his voice is only heard in his head. He is emphasizing each word as if he is new to the English language with slow, deep cadence. "Day one- Welcome! Take a well-earned rest and get excited for the wildlife viewing experience of your life!"

He furrows his brow, not particularly thrilled with the thought of a rainforest safari. As his eyes scan the page his mind flashes back to the day he was watching TV, a day like any other. Then a newsflash comes across the screen "Breaking News". The screen changes to an unsteady image of a visibly shaken cop searching a home. The scene zooms in on two bodies, unmoving. Too still, almost doll like. The camera cuts and zooms in, they are the corpses of his child and his wife sitting in a living room. Set to seem as if watching TV. His eyes glass over as shock sets in. TV has the live feed of the news as cops find the grisly scene. The scene cuts to the police yelling at the news crew to get out and leave some respect for the dead. An officer outside their residence begs the network newscaster not to show the footage until the families have been notified. He tries to stand but the earth is no longer stable he falls down to his knees.

51.

Elemental is typing at his computer, reaching out to his upcoming guests. "I am truly looking forward to everyone coming. This will be our inaugural trip, men. This is an honor I would not bestow on just anybody. I believe that we will find this cathartic and your wound will be healed upon your return. As I am sure you read when you signed the agreements, privacy is our utmost concern."

"I had you all sign nondisclosure agreements. Think of this as a private sanctuary. I take our guests' well-being very seriously. Nothing discussed on this trip will leave the walls of the compound. If anyone feels that they may find issue with this, please know that I will refund you your money and you will still be able to participate in the online group. Does anyone have any questions or concerns? Please voice them now, or hold your peace".

52.

The night sky is changing from murky black to an opalescent blue in the predawn hours. Black Escalades pull up in front of each man's house. This will be the beginning of the next chapter for them. A soulful journey that will bring closure to the heinous hell they have endured by no choice of their own.

They enter the vehicles, climbing in as the shadows slowly start to dissipate in the rising sun. The drivers stow the bags, each performing the exact task methodically in sync even though they are separated by thousands of miles.

Silence from the drivers as the engines start and the trip begins. In what seems like seconds but may have been hours each of the Escalades pull into private hangers at local airports.

The drivers lead them to their own decadent Learjet 60X. An attendant brings them food and a drink. They settle in for the long journey. Being provided with all of the amenities of 5 star travel experience they start to relax allowing the liquor and the opulence to sooth their

Day turns to evening and the sun begins its descent over the water. The planes are landing within a quarter hour of each other. A mere fifteen minutes could as well have been days. Never do the paths of the men cross. They are completely alone with the only human contact being the banal chatter of the flight crew or the silent nods of the drivers. Once again a black Escalade appears to take them to the final destination of their journey.

They drive through a short jungle path, the dirt has been compressed enough to be safe yet the bumps and sway prove certain that they are in a rural area. In front of them appears a metal gate.

The driver opens his window and sets his chin on a device almost identical to an optician's retinal scanner. A code is entered, the scan commences in matter of seconds the iris scan is completed. The gate disappears as the cars pull around the mountain, climbing the steep grade ascent until they come to the lodge.

Large timber trusses and log walls. Old growth logs, the diameter minimum of thirty inches each. The scale of the building compared to the isolation and wildlife surrounding it was a juxtaposed to a tree growing in Brooklyn. Just as out of place yet just as rooted and permanent. The drivers opened the doors as each passenger exited their respective vehicles. The hosts led them inside where they were greeted with beverages and warm smiles. The interior of the behemoth structure was composed of industrial metals and large screen HDTV and computer stations. Walls made of glass that shot up three stories afforded views of the landscape all around. The men are starting to mingle as the lights slowly go down. Elemental appears, but only as an image on the screens strategically located in the building. He is in partial silhouette, backlit and blurred.

"Welcome. So glad you could join us. As you can see, you have arrived to a secure, technologically advanced natural oasis where you will exorcise all of the demons that have been holding you back from living the rest of your life."

The men stand silent, looking at a TV in front of them.

"We will be having our first meeting after lunch. Relax, feel free to explore. We will convene in the great room at two-thirty sharp. Everything you need for the excursions will be provided for you. You are all comfortable with technology, that's a fact. In order for you to get the full immersion experience you will be inculcated with the special equipment and programs that have been incorporated for your total mind, body and spirit experience." With that the screens go dark, Elemental disappears. The men are shown to their rooms by their concierge.

53.

The suites have a living room couch, with furniture made of dark mahogany and white linen. The huge Casablanca fans slowly undulating to circulate the air. Large screen TV's are hidden by canvas paintings of serenity ocean scenes. The top quality latest technology computers, video games and electronic equipment are waiting at ones beck and call. French doors open leading to a large bedroom with a California king bed, overstuffed featherbed and down quilts. The balconies overlook the forest with the turquois colored ocean framing the background.

A stack of newspapers is lying on the coffee tables in all of the rooms. Each paper specifically tailored to the guest in that room.

Michael sits down on the stark white couch and immediately thinks to himself that it could possibly be the softest thing he has ever felt. He picks up one of the papers and is horrified by what he sees. Every paper on the table contains stories about the crime against his family. The headlines are of his wife's death, the kids when they went missing. Articles going back months and months all of the follow ups, op-eds, front page headlines. The stories featuring him and Merl, the stories that made them into monsters or victims, the stories that screamed they deserved it, it was their fault or that they were part of Gods plan. Michael dropped them into the trash. He was revolted and felt nauseous.

He went to lay down, trying to wrap his head round what kind of sick fucking game he has signed up to play. He grabbed the remote and turned on the TV. The one channel was a typical welcome to the hotel channel. The next was a news channel. He settled on this momentarily until the chilling realization of a familiar voice penetrated him. It was the reporter from one of the major networks back home. "Breaking News... Two children gone missing from Yosemite National Park. Believed to be foul play. All law enforcement agencies have been notified. This is an Amber Alert."

Michael turns the channel his hands are shaking and he is fumbling to stop the insidious voice coming from the TV. He finally turns the channel to see another reporter, this time from a national news network that had covered his story. "It's been twenty hours since the Mitchell children have last been seen. There are no signs of the children. The first forty-eight hours are the most vital to the investigation. We will keep you posted. Back to you Deirdre."

Images of Michael and Merleigh appear on the TV in front of Michael. He can't turn away, tears are burning down his cheeks.

Merl is pleading to the cameras during one of the news conferences. She is crying. "Please, if you have our babies... we will do whatever you want. I beg you, money, whatever, we will get it to you." By now she is sobbing with her chest heaving, short of breath, "Just bring Joe and Jilly home. Please... please... please." The reporter continues on as Michaels puts a protective arm around his wife. "The parents requested if you have any information about the children to contact your local law enforcement agency at once -- or please call the National Center for Missing and Exploited Children."

Michael turns the channel only to be confronted by another news clip about the missing kids.

The five o'clock news leads off with "It's been two weeks since Joseph and Jillian Mitchell were last seen. Local authorities are calling off the search...." the screen fades from the anchors to a shot of rescuers searching the forest and surrounding areas with dogs dissolves to a live press conference. Michael and Merleigh looked so haggard and despondent, Eric standing by their side, dutiful and stalwart.

This time Michael takes the mic. "We have not given up hope that Joe and Jilly will be returned to us unharmed. We have trust in God that he will return them safe and we pray that will be any minute."

Merl whimpers, it's now her turn to speak. "Joe Joe, Jilly Bean -- Mamma and Daddy are right here. We love you, ya hear, we love you so much. Stay strong babies, Mamma's never..." she takes a jagged breath, trying to control her raging emotions, "...never, never gonna let..." She is losing herself and the world has a front row seat. Her nose is raw and running, her makeup is cried off. She is clutching the blanket that the kids used the last time we saw them.

"...anything ever happen..." She is starting to hyperventilate. "...to you." The press conference ends with her in pure hysterics, looking out as if they were sitting in the audience of blood thirsty reporters, "Mamma and Daddy love you!!"

With that she turns to the camera, frenzied, violent "You son of a bitch!" She grabs the camera turning her anger and rage to it as if it was the thing that stole her children from under her. "Bring my babies back! Bring em back! Please... bring... them..." With that she drops to her knees, so despondent, so beaten and numb, "... back... to... me!!"

Eric consoles the distraught couple, arms around both.

Looking impeccable he steps up to the podium. "My clients want to reiterate that there is a $1,000,000 reward for the return of Joe and Jilly Mitchell. If anyone has any information, contact your local law enforcement agency at once or please call the National Center for Missing and Exploited Children."

Michael confused and nauseous, not sure what to make of the barrage of cruel reality he was forced to endure over again. Sweat is dripping from his brow, dripping down the tip of his nose, soaking the nape of his neck through his shirt onto the clean linen sheets. He stood up to turn the TV off and the radio on out of pure disgust and belligerence.

News jockeys on the AM stations are reporting from vans outside his home. "Live at the Mitchell residence. Merleigh Mitchell, age thirty-five, found DOA from an apparent drug overdose. Sources confirm that Merleigh Mitchell was found dead today..."

Michael turns the tuner, hands shaking... This time a female reporter's voice, "No charges have been filed against Michael Mitchell in the untimely death of his wife Merleigh. If you remember, Michael and Merleigh Mitchell's children were abducted while they were on a family vacation at Yosemite National Park. No reported sightings since that tragic day."

Michael turned the radio off. Sitting down on the foot of the bed he puts his head in his hands and cries.

54.

The scene is repeating itself in the room of the man from L.A. He is watching the same flash back broadcasts.

An Asian reporter with a nasal voice reports from the corner of the street where the cantina is. "In another case of teen sex trafficking, a body has been discovered. Following up on a lead from local unnamed sources the body of a young girl was found in a dumpster earlier today. Sources have confirmed this nondescript building housed a local bodega by day, bordello by night." Shot of bordello where the girls were held, tagged with gang graffiti, otherwise nondescript. "The M.E. believes it was an illegal abortion gone terribly wrong. Detectives and SWAT found the second girl who was with the victim at the time of their disappearance. Names withheld due to the age of the victims. Witnesses say the second girl's tongue was removed."

An overweight female witness with a very strong Spanish accent and painted on eyebrows is in the background talking to police. The camera then spans the neighborhood as kids in baggy pants and white wife beaters are sporting colored bandanas on their heads avoiding the cameras but not allowing anything to escape their sight.

The reporter continues "She was found chained to a hot water heater. She is in critical condition. We will keep you posted".

L.A. Man standing in his room with a look of shock, trembling with rage.

55.

The man from New Orleans is in his suite. He is sitting on the edge of his couch with a glass of water in his hand. His hand is shaking so badly the water is splashing and he barely notices it. He can't tear his eyes away from the news reporting in front of him.

Here stands a reporter that is in his mid-fifties clad in a windbreaker and khakis. He is a throwback from the days when the news was the news. He is stoic and he is a straight arrow. He is wearing very little make up for today's HDTV, and the years of reporting on human horrors and tragedies are taking their toll on him clearly evident by the deep lines of a continually furrowed brow. He no longer tries to hide the light accent he has picked up from being in New Orleans for so many years. Today his eyes seem hollow as he reports on the NOLA horror house.

"Missing mother and child found. Horror abounds in this quiet parish. Neighbors reported a stench coming from this picturesque home. What police found was heart-wrenching, even to these seasoned professionals. A mother and her daughter, both dead for some time, set in an eerie tableau of everyday life."

New Orleans Man throws his glass against the wall next to the TV. "What kinda sick prank!?" He turns off the TV and turning on the radio "Breaking news-- Missing family found in morose…" This is his breaking point as he reaches down and rips the digital radio out of the wall.

"What da? Is dis some sick shit!"

56.

The man from New York is settling in. He is showered and wearing the warm soft robe the suite has provided for him. He is enjoying the quiet for a moment. He decides to sit and page through the NY Times and Post and Daily News, not noticing the dates of publication at first.

His eyes scan the front page and spy articles about his daughter. He crumbles the papers in his hand, his face twists with rage, he turns on the TV. A late thirty something blonde blue eyed Ken Doll anchor reports as his dimples soften the depravity of his words. "This is an ABC NY news breaking story. All of America has watched in horror as the cyber world has turned into a dark and gruesome place for one family. The little girl who went missing from her NY home to only appear online on a live feed during her treacherous kidnapping has yet to be found." The shot zooms to a child on the web, his child.

The reporter looks serious yet smiles as he continues, "All resources are being utilized. There is a worldwide bounty hunt for the man who is responsible for the sexual abuse, rape and torture of America's little sweetheart, as well as for those interacting with him via online requests. If anyone has any information, contact the FBI -- they have a special cyber task force -- or call the National Center for Missing and Exploited Children. All call will be kept confidential."

New York picks up the rest of the newspapers, reading the headlines in horror he comes to realize this is planned. He squeezes the newspapers in his hands until his knuckles turn white he crumbles them and throws them in the trash.

"Who are you? You sick son of a bitch?" He is running through the room like a caged zoo animal. He looks into the corners of the room trying to see if he is being watched.

57.

TV's turn on synchronously with a clear view inside the guest suites. Each man is repeating the same steps to the same dance in their own rhythm and their own way. Elemental is pleased with how easily human behavior can be manipulated to get a decided outcome. Switching to each of the men watching the TV at the same time, elemental takes control of their TV's and once again appears backlit on their TV screens, a partial silhouette. "By now you have had a chance to settle in. I am sure that you have many questions."

Each man stop motionless turning to the TV in their room.

"Please gentlemen, I assure you that everything that you are experiencing is for you own good. Trust me, friends -- you are safe here. I promise you, anything that happens while you are here will never leave here."

New York Man tries to turn off the TV but the remote no longer works.

Elemental continues in a warm stern voice, "You have total immunity and protection from any outside interference. Believe me gentlemen when I tell you that all of this is for your own wellbeing. You will understand why you have to experience what you are experiencing. It is a process my friends, and I am here to help you."

"Please be in the Great Room on the main floor in forty-five minutes. Cocktails and appetizers will be served. In the meantime call your concierge if there is anything we can do for you. Good day." With that the TV screens went black, and each man was left to process the events of the day, for now.

58.

All guests are collecting in the great room. The imposing height of the vaulted ceilings, the sheer size of the wooden log beams make everything in comparison feel very small and insignificant by design. The mid afternoon sun filtering through the smoke colored windows gave everything a shadowy affect.

The men stood silently eyeing one another, their distrust apparent and totally understandable after the earlier occurrences of the day. No one spoke a word, worried of how they may appear to the others, not quite sure of anything at the moment, but especially whom or what they should trust including themselves.

Soon, as the men have their drinks and time starts to move on they begin to interact. Beginning with daily niceties of who, what where and placing a name or location to the face.

Elemental appears on a balcony overlooking the great room, overlooking his guests. Unnoticed yet in plain sight he watches the interactions of the men below.

Not noticing that the staff is herding the groups of certain men together, Michael, New Orleans, New York and LA are now congregating in close proximity. In a short time they are interacting, starting to feel comfortable with each other, building on their on-line relationships. The New Orleans man can no longer hold back and starts to ask the question that has been on the tip of the collective tongue,

"Hey, did ya 'all have anyting tricky happen to you since you been here?"

They all nod in unison as each man retells his story.

New York, "I was sitting in my room…" He tells of the gruesome pictures flashing before him on the TV, of his young daughter performing unspeakable acts in front of millions of salacious predators bidding for her every move.

L.A. "I turned on the radio to hear the reports…" He relates the story of the botched abortion and the beatings and rapes. How the pictures in the paper were of his daughter with a black bar across her face, the bloody rag shoved in her mouth to soak up the blood from where her tongue once was.

New Orleans, "Rotten Sommabitch replayed every news cast wit ma baby girl and her momma, what that fucka did…" The way he felt the day the news was broken, how his heart dropped out of his chest as the world fell away from beneath his feet.

59.

The room darkened, and a spotlight went to the balcony where Elemental had watched from the shadows. Taking his place centered in the soft beam of the filtered light he spread his arms in a welcoming warm gesture. From speakers located in what felt like every stationary object in the room his voice boomed "Welcome, welcome. We have some exciting things to cover. I am so elated to see you all here. We are going to start by introducing ourselves. Gentlemen, for your protection and serenity you will be known by location only and cause of your journey."

Elemental stood taking in the quizzical looks underscored by contemplative rage and fury. The energy in the room was palpable, but not quite where he was hoping for it to be. He looked at the small group of men, well outnumbered by the staff, smiling a somewhat subversive smile and putting his hands together as if praying, fingertip to fingertip and continued with his introduction.

"Remember, anonymity please. Why don't we start geographically? East Coast?"

New York Man looking from face to face, obviously nervous, distrustful. "I guess you all know why I am here. I am from the city. I, uh, I'm from New York. Sorry, sometime we forget that there is more than one city in the world besides ours."

Nervous laughter from the crowd.

He continued mouth dry, voice husky from the tightening muscles in his throat. "Anyways, I got in touch wit Elemental on the web site after my kid disappeared. I've been on there for a few months. Trying to keep my sanity…"

Stir of agreement from men and staff could be heard and felt.

"Ya know, the press is your best friend, than they're your worst enemy. See, my kid was the one that was all over the web."

The crowd falls silent.

"The one where pervs were I-IM'ing what to do to her?"

The crowd nods with a low tone in agreement.

"There wasn't a place I could go and not see my kid. The news people all actin' like they care just to get the first scoop on the story. My kid ain't a story. She was my daughter..." He looked down and away, turning slightly away from the crowd as one would to protect themselves from a pounding sideways rain. This was the first time he had referred to his girl as was and it hit him like a cement wall.

Room welcomes him with a round of soft applause.

New Orleans was standing away from crowd, looking down at floor. He is opening and closing his hands, staring at a small pull in the carpet, his eyes burning a hole into the floor. He stands silent for a moment, then looks at the faces of the four men standing around him, and finally up at Elemental who nods in encouragement. He starts to speak, almost inaudible as the pain permeated his nerve endings.

"I came down heya from Orleans. Ya see, I was workin' late, so ma wife and girl went for suppa and never came back. At furst, I was tinkin' she went and left. I loved her, but I wadn't perfect. So I went over to da next parish, callin in on her family, hopin to get them to talk to her for me. Nuh, uh, afta talkin' to her momma, I knew sumptin was bad. Started prayin' when I didn't hear from 'em by late night. Then I called the po-lice."

Rubbing the back of his neck, obviously not comfortable with the amount of information he is sharing. "Dey said dat sint it was bote of dem dey'd get right on it. Then men and women from all ov-da globe came. Big ol' mob in front of ma house. Offerin' me da silver dime if I told dem what I knew fuhst. Well, afta a while the wuhld seemed to fuhget bout us. I kept tryin' to find da gurls, but nuttin I did seemed to help, nuttin."

He searched from man to man, seeing that each of them understood him, probable knew him betta than he knew hiself at this point.

"Afta what seemed a long time, I'm sitting watchin' da news and I see dis reporter dat looked familiar. She said dey had word on da missing family from da city…"

He started swaying left to right, barely noticeable. His hands traveled along the nape of his neck, his chin so low it almost touched his chest. He was now back in that room, he had traveled back to the very minute of discovery.

"I sat der tinkin' dis can't be. Dear God, can dis be? If the po-leece had sumtin dey would had said it to me furst. I watched as da TV people started showin' muh girls. Lookin' like they was some play dolls. Hair and makeup dun did, sittin' in dat livin' room, dressed up in those weird clothes, looking like wax doll versions of demselves. I thought it wad a replica of dem, like someone recreated the scene from da news? Sum sick bastids out dere, ya know?"

He nervously switched his weight under the scrutiny of his peers from left to right, swaying now like he was on a barge on the Mississippi, only to realize it wasn't scrutiny, but empathy. He connected to the men with a chin check or a slight nod of agreement.

"Next ting I know the po-leece are knockin on ma house. Dey got some news dey need to tell me. I slammed da dore on em, I'd seen what dey was here to tell me, I'd seen and heard nuff ready. I slammed dat dore, I leaned against it trying to hold da wurl out, if I don't answer, it ain't real, ya know? Nuttin been the same sint. Da trial was a hot mess. People accusin', actin' as if it was der family. Guess this is the last rope I'm gunna be given befo I can't hang on anymo."

The L.A. Man squares shoulders, suppressing his rage from the welcome he received in his room. He begins his introduction with a slight nervous stutter from emotion and adrenaline that have this ex-marine holding fast to the break point.

"Left coast, L.A. Got to m-my room, received one helluva welcome. Head trip? I didn't know this was some sick fucking j-joke. Sorry guys, I can't believe none of you had the huevos to say anything!"

Elemental was right on cue, "Keep calm everyone. I will explain that in a minute. Please just relax and realize that nothing is done to hurt you, it is all part of the process. Go on. Please, go on."

Distrustful, yet apprehensive from being out of his element, the L.A. Man reluctantly tells his story.

"M-my meja and her best friend were at that age, ya know? Looking to act grown? I knew there were issues in my neighborhood, but they n-never affected any of us. We are hard-working class, honest folks. It was just a day. That d-day that changed everything forever."

Crowd murmurs in agreement.

"The girls wanted to g-go on their own. They wanted to go for a hike. Looking like a TV commercial, all done in pony tails and our pit bull ready. They had painted the dog's nails pink that day, and put a big fluffy scarf on her neck. I remember, I tried not to laugh as the trio came in to ask me if they could go. She leaned over, smelling like grape bubble gum and coconut shampoo, putting her arms around my neck she said," for this he whispered as if reciting sacred text, "Poppy, you know I love you, with that she g-gave m-me an extra tight squeeze and I gave her a huge bear h-hug and off they went. N-never came home. I had heard stories they grew pot up there in the hills behind us. Urban legends never paid it much thought."

Looking down, trying to flash an artificial smile to hide the sudden surge of emotions.

"I th-thought, well I never believed that violence would spill to here. My cousins in Mexico tell me stories, now it happened to us. Cops, family, neighbors, suspicion, questions, n-no sleep, arguments, depression, b-blame, anger, rage, it never ends. After what I guess would be forever, some g-guy d-dumpster diving found her. M-my daughter's best friend-- a bloody cold lump thrown out with the t-trash. M-m-my angel, m-my everything was tied up and her tongue cut out. M-my sweet meja. The guilt eating m-me up... I- I'm not sure if she would have b-been b-better off dead then live with this forever?!"

Voice shaky, cracking, as he tears up. His muscles tensing and relaxing like a Boa Constrictor under his tight fitting shirt. The arteries in his temple and his neck pulsating as the memories become more and more vivid.

"What kind of a man secretly wishes his daughter dead?'

While the other men stood telling their stories, Michael melted into the background, only catching a word or a phrase. The room was spinning. He knew what was expected of him, he had to tell his tale of woe next. Dear God, help me summon the strength to get through this…

60.

Prisoners returned to their cells. They had been beaten, tortured both mentally and physically. They had lost track of time and reality. They had shreds of humanity that they were grappling to hold onto, but those were dissipating fast.

They were acclimating to their cells, damp, dark, moldy, dank, and cold, which after the extraordinary pain they had endured seemed luxurious. They were served warm broth, a piece of bread and some fruit that was minutes away from putrefying. Eating what constituted real meals for the first time in weeks was glorious, until they realized the excruciating pain from having solid food travel their shrunken digestive tract. The cramping, the hot knife of agony caused by the raid expansion of a starved belly, yet they continued to eat, acting on pure instinct. For most, they no longer thought about anything, no memories, no planning for the future, they were on pure survival mode.

All except for one.

61.

Elemental turns and gestures towards Michael, "Well, it looks like we have one last introduction."

He opens his hand, motioning to Michael.

62.

On the set of a national talk show in Chicago. The audience if filled with Midwestern housewives on a girls day trip to the "city" and people who have flown in from one corner of the globe or another just to take part of the media empire and breathe the same air as their idol. Kione sits on the sound stage, turning on the charm with his half smile and genuine glance to one audience member or another. He is perched, dressed business casual, on a velvet couch. The producers are holding up signs to laugh and clap. None of this particularly fazes Kione, except when he needs to be self-deprecating, that act is a little harder to pull off, but he masters it artfully.

He is telling his story of how he became the monster he is today. The host is a Wendy Williams type- a relatable likeable woman. The show is in mid-interview.

The host reaffixes her mic onto deep cut purple Diane Von Furstenberg. Five, four, three, two, and the set manager points his fingers without missing a beat the host continues on. "One thing we can't seem to understand... You seem to be the type of boy every mother would want her son to be. You are handsome, articulate and you seem to have a gentle demeanor. What went wrong, darling, and where?

Kione looks at her sheepishly, flashing beautiful white teeth and a bashful grin. "Why, thank you ma'am. I tried to fight those demons that were inside me. When I was a young man, about the age of those kids… Well, my dad…You see, I worshipped my daddy. He was my hero.

The host leans over, grabbing his wrist and looks deep into his doe eyes, "That's the way it should be."

He bites his lip gently, appearing to be fighting back a wave of emotions, "Well, my mom left and Dad blamed it on me. We were wealthy-- beyond. He was a marketing psychiatrist. Companies would pay him millions of dollars to get into their customers' heads. My dad… It's weird saying Dad, after my mom left he made me call him J.E. Sorry..

"That's alright, is that when everything started to turn for the worst son?"

Kione looked to be fighting back tears, he nodded, wiped his eye with the back of his wrists and continued "J.E. Norwood otherwise known as my father, the man could do anything and it didn't matter. He has friends in government, business and military. He was originally a Pentagon psychiatrist."

The cameras pan the audience of stay at home moms and kids off from college. The females are trying to catch Kiones eye, hoping to connect even momentarily with this poor boyish man they think may need saving, a few of them subconsciously flirting with him.

Kione is relatable and every word he speaks is so heartfelt that it leaves the audience on the edge of their seats with baited breath, hanging on for dear life as he relates this tragic fairytale.

"My father was adept at mixing physical and psychological torture. Locking me in the closet, or locking me outside with no clothes except my undershorts, not even shoes after I would get out of the shower he would make me wake up and take in the middle of the night during winter."

The audience gasped, and the host knew her ratings were skyrocketing with each and every syllable he spoke. She was his first, and from what she understood, his only interview before he got sentenced to death. "Oh my, that is terrible. How did you manage? You were so young to have gone through something so harsh."

"The longer my mom was away, the worse it got. Putting me in the shower and electroshocking me, tying me to the bed. Using a razor to make little cuts in every fold of my body..."

Kione pauses, lifts up his shirt, showing a perfect six pack, as the camera zooms in for a close up lines of scars come into focus, showing a hounds-tooth pattern barely visible but certainly real covering his taught skin.

"I would scream and cry and he told me if I became a man my mother would come back. I wasn't sure what being a man meant, but..."

The host inhaled sharply, audibly in disgust, shock, and compassion for a human being who had such a horrible life. "Ladies and Gentlemen, this is why we need to stop abuse before it the story end tragically like this one did. Kione is not responsible for living in a sadistic, cruel home during his formative years. The man on trial should really be his father!"

Kione eyed her like she was his salvation. He sat a little straighter in his seat and spoke directly to the audience and the camera, emotion oozing from his lips, drawing out a tear from the jaded cameraman.

"He would act like he was doing me a favor. Well, over time, things got worse -- 'til one day I was able to get out. I lived on my own, with only these horrible thoughts in my head to keep company. I was scared of what I was capable of. I would pretend that I was doing all of those things to the monster that hurt me. But, the longer I was alone, the more real the monsters became, and the stronger the urge to actually perform these acts of living thing."

His leg started to shake, and the host gently put her had on it to calm him as he went on. "Thoughts of my father just disappeared. I never heard of him again. If he wanted me he had the resources and connections to find me."

A few audience members let a boo or two escape from them, some were sobbing, others tsk tsking.

"I am sure someone probably killed him. I only wish it was me. Then I may not have had to do all the horrible things that I did."

The audience murmurs and inhales audibly with the reference to Michael's children.

"My father, he was friends with some very evil people. One day, the two just showed up, out of thin air." Kione starts to sob, shoulders moving up and down.

"So Kione, tell us, was it impulse. Tell us that you didn't plan to go out and do this?"

Kione looks out into the sea of faces. Some of the faces now showing the fear that this too could happen to their children too, he reads them, he knows how to get their sympathy...

"I can't explain it. It was like a volcano erupted- all the rage that was building for years, all those thoughts in my head. I took a minute and imagined the normal life I was meant to have but I knew it was too late. I knew I was wrong, but I just couldn't stop it. I just couldn't stop it. Then once I started, well then I started to enjoy it. It became like a video game. Nothing was real. Like I was just playing a game, and I could create or destroy anything in my game, I finally had control." He curled his full, wet lips into a smile so sweet it was almost cherubic and began to laugh maniacally.

63.

Michael looks out into the room of faces, clenches his fists ready to tell his story.

"I am from the North Coast of California. I ran my own consulting firm. I had a beautiful wife, two kids and a dog. Livin' the dream. We decided to go on a nature vacation. Bring the family closer, ya know. Get away from the rats and the race they make us run."

As he talks, he feels as if he is traveling back through time and space-- back to the sounds...water rushing, birds singing, the rustle of leaves.

The sound of Merleigh screaming...

He is reiterating the facts robotically "On a getaway. One minute life was rolling along, couldn't be better, next, time just stopped. My daughter Jilly and my son Joe were kidnapped. We were only a few feet away. We couldn't do a damn thing. I became obsessed with finding them and my wife became clinically depressed. She ended up taking her own life with happy pills. A few months ago, their remains were found. The bastard..." Michael clenches his jaw; enraged at the anticlimactic ending to the repellant, sadistic, sexually perverse crimes that were committed. "...that did it-- he just shrugged his shoulders, smiled and gave a wink to the cameras. Meanwhile they found a torture chamber in his home."

Elemental cut Michael off, "Can we have a round of applause? You are all brave men, who faced unspeakable circumstances and made it through to the other side. This is the final element to your healing process. The last ingredient to your return to living the life you were meant to lead. As you all know, I believe that regaining power and control over your demons is the key. Please look up at the screen closest to you."

The Plasma 3D TVs all turn on, the screens showing a virtual land identical to the lodge and the island appear. A CGI replica of every person in the room every member of staff, all appearing in this realistic virtual reality in front of them so surreal it gave Michael gooseflesh.

"Gentlemen, you may notice certain similarities. We are about to embark on a scientific breakthrough. I am pleased to announce that I am offering you a very unique opportunity that people around the world would give their lives for. I am offering you the chance to take revenge on those who have stolen your lives and loved ones from you. If you will follow me, we will be going to the Arcade.

L.A. Man speaks in a hushed tone to the man next to him. "W-what? I did n-not just hear him just say we flew halfway round the world to play video games?"

New York Man speaks to no one and everyone at the same time. The crowd is showing some dissent... "What the... ya gotta be fuckin kiddin me. Excuse me, but the last fuckin thing I need to do is have anything to do with a God Damn computer. I spent a shit load of coin to get myself here, and we're gonna be playing games on a fuckin computer?!?!? Excuse me..." He looks up to elemental as the group is passing through the archway underneath the balcony he is standing on. "Hey you, up there! Were you one of the twisted fucks making requests on line? You better get me the fuck outta here before I decide to make you a fuckin poster child for displaced anger management."

New York Man turns toward the door, and the men start to become uneasy. Elemental hurriedly tries to regain control. The assistants block his departure.

Elemental responds, as soothing as if he were cooing to a baby, "That's fair. I understand that you may feel apprehensive, but it truly is in your best interest to at least see what it is about. Trust men. We can trust one another, implicitly. You will understand incrementally. It is too much for a person to take in at once. Everything will be revealed, due time."

With obvious apprehension the men proceed to the arcade. Not able to place their trust into Elemental but the thought of getting past their tortured history to a brighter future much weighed more important than the nagging apprehension they all felt.

64.

Once the men enter the arcade they find themselves in a media room equipped with luxurious leather chairs, gaming headgear and ear buds. This state of the art gaming room was designed for total immersion play.

Elemental appears on a balcony overlooking the arcade. "Gentlemen please find a chair. You will notice that each station has been equipped with the highest quality gear. I have had this specially designed for your senses to be completely submerged into the game. If you will gear up, the staff is here to assist you with the equipment."

The staff, beautiful robotic young men and women walk around gearing up each man. The men are intrigued yet dismayed and seriously uncomfortable from the impending doom that lurks around every corner. Drawing from the previous experiences in their rooms earlier in the day, they are hesitant even pensive.

Elemental waits as the final equipment is put in place. "Wonderful, you are geared up and the experience will begin. Don't be nervous. I have designed the game to be completely interactive with the staff. If -- at any time -- you should need something, you do not have to stop the game. The equipment is wireless. Once you log on and are fitted, the game will only stop for meals and rest. From now until the quest, you are to be geared at all times. This is in preparation for your final extrication. Are there any questions?"

L.A. Man closely looking at the gear through his Google glasses he turns to his assistant, "Yo -- this is some weird sh-shit." He looks up and raises his hand, his voice directed to Elemental.

"You asked us if we got questions. Hell yeah, I got some questions. I don't g-get how this is g-gonna get rid of my n-night terrors. I don't see how pretending to be some game nerd is gonna do a damn bit of good. What I really don't get is why we" turning around, sweeping his hands indicating the inclusion of the rest of the men, "were forced to see every piece of media coverage. Why were we m-made to relive it? Yeah, if you could just answer those..."

All men murmur in agreement.

65.

Inside the prison bunker there is no sign of natural light, nothing to indicate time. The prisoners being told they have almost completed their truncated sentences via hidden audio system...

An electronic voice comes over an intercom system, "Men, in twenty-four hours you will be set free. Congratulations. Only a select few were chosen for this experiment. It is up to you, after sunrise tomorrow to leave here and start the rest of your lives with a clean slate. You will no longer be fugitives you will have paid you debts to society in full. Thank you for being willing participants I certainly hope that we will never cross paths again."

66.

The men, dressed in the gaming gear are becoming belligerent. Elemental deals with this mini revolt, he was surprised that it took them this long.

"Gentlemen, I understand your reservations! I am glad that you finally asked." He responded to the men's questions about the incidents in their rooms, contentedly purring as if he were getting a massage while talking to the group. "It is imperative that you allow all the feelings that you have been repressing to surface. You will find that in the end every step is crucial and justified. You will fight the good fight. Just open yourself, and you will find places inside of you to draw strength and courage to do things, things which you never thought possible."

Elemental begins the decent down the massive log steps into the center of the room. He turns, eyeing each man, making the final adjustments himself to their uniforms. The men wearing the headpieces, from their perspectives they are dressed in full military garb. The line is completely blurred between what is real and what is part of the game and what is reality.

Elemental paces between each man, like a drill sergeant. "Accuracy and attention to detail men, this is crucial to your healing and your wellbeing. Men- from this point on this is not a game! Everything is calculated precisely to fit and the plan is to be executed with such exactitude, such attention to detail, such foresight to each element that it will go as easily and seamlessly as taking a deep breath. Is everyone good with that?"

The group signals their agreement.

"OK then. Shall we get started? First, I will ask you to go to your rooms and proceed with your day as you would have before you were fitted. I think you are getting the idea about what to expect. Meet here in an hour. If there are any glitches to the system, it is better we fix them now. Is that clear, men?"

Michael finds himself responding as if he were a military recruit. "Yes sir."

L.A. snaps "Roger that"

"Uh huh." Comes pensively from New York

 "Ya huh, Crystal." Growls New Orleans

The rest of the men follow in agreement as the leave the great room and veer off into separate direction back to their rooms.

67.

Back in his suite Michael looks about, apprehensive after the welcome he had received. Talking to himself out loud... "Well, at least I am prepared for whatever they throw my way. That last little stunt just about freaked the shit out of me. Bring it on."

Moving to sit and relax in the living quarters he sees pictures of Merl, Joe and Jilly. Pictures he has not seen in ages. He picks them up, holding them to his chest. He starts to talk to them while looking at the one of him and Merl on their first getaway together.

"You know, I am doing this for you, dontcha?" he whispers "I gotta get out of this place in my head. It's really dark and if I don't- well, I'm not sure what I'm capable of anymore. I know you're with me. I know you can hear me. Please tell me, am I doing the right thing?"

*

New York is sitting on bed, looking at photos of his family from happier times. Picking up each picture and closing his eyes and putting it down as if imprinting the memory forever into his mind. "Oh my baby, Daddy really let you down. How could I have let this happen to you? I promised you I would always keep the monsters away. I broke that promise and in turn it broke me. I wasn't worth being your Daddy. But to me you will always be my little girl. You are still my angel. I love you so much. I wish I could take it all back. I wish I could make him suffer the same way he made you suffer. Oh, my angel, I am so sorry."

*

New Orleans paces, looking at photos of his family from happier times. He grabs at his wife's scarf and daughter's teddy bear. Bringing them up to his face and inhaling their essence. "My Cheri and muh petit bebe. I let you so down. I wudn't the man I thought I was. I couldn't even keep y'all safe. Cher, I waited, I called, I prayed. For a time I thought you dun walked up and out on me. I am so so sorry. Minutes and hours I wasted. May be if we coulda done sumtin different. I tink it may be time Cheri. Sumtin led me heeya, da reason is I tink yo had sumtin to do with dat. I know I can't go conjuring you for an answer, but I pray that you and our bebe will lead me in the right way."

*

L.A. is standing at the door between the bedroom and living room in the suite. Not believing all of the mementos from his past that appeared here. Clutching his crucifix saying a silent prayer on his knees... "Dear God, I am sorry I seem to only c-call on you lately when I am in trouble, But I fear I have made a t-terrible m-mistake coming here." He feels so small even though his appearance is anything but with his muscular shoulders, tattoo sleeve wearing only jeans and a tank. "I have a very bad feeling about this place. Dear God, Please help m-me through this. I beg of you, in the Name of Jesus Christ. Please, please, please help me. I should have relied on you all along. I need you to g-get me through this and home. I need to g-get home to m-my Girl. She needs me God, please let me g-get back to my poor little m-mija. She needs her Poppy m-more now than ever. She needs me, God. Me to make her feel beautiful! Make her feel safe. Take way all the dirty and make her innocent again."

68.

Prisoners are starting to feel rambunctious. There is nothing left to lose. They made it, and now they are full of adrenaline and zest for a life free from the scrutiny of the law.

*

Back at the lodge all the TV's turn on in each room. Replaying the gruesome scenes from each crime on a continuous loop, the men are forced to re-experience the worst moments of their lives. Suddenly, through their ear buds each man is instructed to open the file that has been left outside of their doors. As they do so they see it is a copy of the crime reports. Pictures and forensic explanations all included.

New Orleans opens his, looks at the contents and drops it to the floor. "God forgive me. I hate him. God I hate him! If I had the chance, dear God, I'd kill 'im then skin him. Make him pay for what he did to my bebes. God, I'm gonna crack." He paces like a caged animal becoming more aggressive. "I can' take it anymore. I hate him. I hate him, I hate him!" He is pumping his clenched fists, his blood pressure rising, his breathing becoming jagged spitting into the mic as he screams into the air.

*

New York looks at the file, inhaling sharply as he finds the courage to look at the paperwork. He spreads out the contents onto the bed and examines them with precision and a focus he had no idea he possessed. Placing them methodically from the bed and organizing them on the floor and the desk. He configures the evidence into makeshift shrine. He holds the mug shot to his heart, "It may not be today, but I will give you exactly what you deserve."

*

L.A. Man retrieves his package with his right hand remaining attached to his crucifix. "I don't need to be reminded. I don't need to have it in my face. Oh, Santa Maria, how can you allow this?" He is physically anguished. "I live with it every day! What can I do?" He grabs his Bible, and starts to read from Exodus. He flashes backs to the girls being tortured coinciding with each bible verse.

"These are the laws you are to set before us: Anyone who strikes a man and kills him shall surely be put to death." He imagines the greasy men raping his daughter and her best friend.

"But if a man schemes and kills another man deliberately, take him away from my altar and put him to death" He can see them holding his daughter down as she fights, they use forceps to open her mouth into an inhuman position.

"Anyone who kidnaps another and either sells him or still has him when he is caught must be put to death." He hears her screaming, crying as they show her her own tongue. Than they take turn spitting into her open bloody mouth.

"If men who are fighting hit a pregnant woman and she gives birth prematurely but there is no serious injury, the offender must be fined whatever the woman's husband demands and the court allows." The dirty bastards who sodomized the girls one last time before they performed the massacre abortion with bleach and a coat hanger.

"But if there is serious injury, you are to take – life for life, an eye for eye, tooth for tooth, hand for hand, foot for foot, burn for burn, wound for wound, bruise for bruise. Gracias Santa Maria, you have answered my prayers." Kissing his crucifix he places it back inside his shirt.

*

Michael takes the evidence packet back to the couch. He pours himself a whiskey on the rocks. This is the first drink he's had in a few days, and at this point he knows he deserves it. Looking down he realizes that he has been staring at this same envelope for months. Eric had given to him to look over and he had placed it in the back of Merls closet. He never brought himself to look at the contents.

"I just want to go home. I am so tired. Please... I don't care anymore. The only thing left in my heart is hate and rage. I can't stop thinking every waking moment about what I would do, if given the chance, to Kione."

He sat with the unopened envelope on his lap.

69.

Elemental is sitting in his office, smoking a cigar and smiling looking at the wall of TV screens from the security system in front of him. The entire island is wired with CC TV, an electronic eye watching the prisoners, the guests and the staff.

The men started a strict boot camp style regimen of physical training- detoxifying in the saunas, running for miles through the sticky jungles, being woken up in the middle of the night for therapy sessions while their subconscious was still accessible.

This unrelenting routine ran straight for five days, pushing them to their braking points and bringing them back from the brink. The few minutes of peace when they escaped back to their rooms were filled with reminders of why they were here. Pictures, newspapers, TV clips, evidence, voices of friends and family, a constant barrage of physical and mental barbs and assaults to their sanity. As alliances started to form, the men were separated from the group to what was referred to as solitary reflection.

Elemental watched from his perch, making notes, coordinating as if he were a movie producer. Setting scenes, editing locations, the most menial details were under his control. He took a seat on his pony skin couch, leaned back and watched his masterpiece in motion.

"Things could not be coming together any better. With planning, forethought and inspiration one can accomplish anything they set out to do. Oh, how I wish I could share this moment." A tear runs down his cheek. "I did this for you, my dear boy. I did all of this for you. I hope you finally understand."

70.

In the large industrial kitchen the staff is getting ready to serve dinner. Ostrich steaks, king crab legs a feast fit for kings.

The dining staff servers are as exotic as the setting. The women are examples of physical perfection dressed in black halter dresses. The front a puddle of black satin plunging just north of the naval and the length just a hair below indecency, backless with a single gold chain hanging down the length of the spine stopping directly center of the Dimple of Venus. They wear gold stilettos, the only undergarment is the bronzer they wear on their legs and down the décolletage, their fingernails are manicured to offset the cinnamon tone of their skin, everything about them oozes sensuality.

As the men prepare for dinner the servers are preparing for the men, dusting their glasses with powder for the post dinner aperitifs.

The men are filing into the dining room. Sitting down to a veritable feast an eerie quiet hangs in the air. They are attempting to process the day's events and information, struggling to prepare for the next move.

The dinner is exquisite. Each course outdoes the last. The meal is succulent and divine obviously prepared by one of the top chefs in the world. Every detail of the meal is designed to seduce all five of the senses.

Elemental stands at the head of the table. He lifts his glass in a toast. "To my friends. You have made such amazing progress. Growth and personal change is painful."

Looking at the face of each man at the table he spoke genuinely directly to them. "Ask the butterfly. No, caterpillars do not simply hide inside their cocoon and after a few days emerge as a butterfly. What happens inside is that the caterpillar releases an enzyme that digests every tissue of the caterpillar. The caterpillar must have it in them to create the metamorphosis."

Clearing his throat he continued, "These transformations, into the wings, legs, organs, and antennae of the butterfly, are painful. During the first four days inside of the cocoon the body, the soul of the caterpillar are dissolved literally into liquid. Then, as if by magic, the cells inside the chrysalis start growing. These cells arrange themselves, forming from a caterpillar into a liquid into to butterfly."

The servers move stealthily, removing dinner plates, leaning over just enough to give the guests something to think about other than the issues at hand. Intentionally brushing the arms and backs of the guests with their chests ever so gently as they serve the cigars and aperitifs. It is tangible sexuality hanging in the air like forbidden fruit.

Elemental lifts his glass, the others follow suit. "My friends, you will soon emerge on the other side. Patience, you will not be sorry. Now, enjoy your dinners. Tomorrow we meet right here at dawn. We have a safari planned. Good night. Cheers!"

The men move to the library, finishing their drinks and lighting their cigars. A haze of cigar smoke wafts to the vaulted ceiling.

Two of the women who were waiting on Elemental take their place standing on the huge table that is centered in the room after the men have found a comfortable seat. They start to dance, leaning back to back, slowly moving up and down. In synch they grab the gold chain of the others dress and the small pieces of material fall away. They turn to face each other, still dancing, but exploring the endless sea of caramel skin in front of them. Playfully the use their mouths and fingers to caress, to stroke, titillate, tease. Soon it is as if they no longer realize they are the center of entertainment for the room around them. The lighter of the two spreads her leg, inviting the other to make a feast out of her glistening, clean shaven mound.

While the show is in progress the other servers approach the guests, offering their services discretely taking a hand and placing it upon her upper thigh, so the tip of a thumb can slide in between very hungry lips, her mouth brushing against his ear, her hot breath burning through him tapping something primal.

Michael's server stands behind him, raking her fingernails through his hair, she slowly moves to his side, moving her index finger softly, purposefully around the collar of his shirt, down the row of buttons and starts fumbling with his belt. He is hard. His tip is poking out of the top of his pants. Helplessly watching the scene unfold in front of him, he is paralyzed.

The women on the table are in ecstasy, rendered helpless by plunging probing fingers into secret places, the smell of perfume and sex intoxicating.

The women have taken total control of the men they are paired with. New York is sitting on the couch, a goddess is standing in front of him with her foot planted squarely on his crotch, moving her hands up and down her bare chest, until she finds her dark cherry colored nipples she pinches and pulls them, leaning in closer and closer until he fights to suck on them but she won't let him. She is moving her foot up and down his crotch, and has managed to unzip his pants with her toes. He is absurdly still as she moves to straddle him. She has finally allowed him access to her.

New Orleans server is standing in front of him as he reaches his hands to her face she takes his fingers in her mouth, slowly licking them, moving her tongue up and down and in between each one sucking on each one, she takes her hands and moves them between her legs, moaning as she moves them expertly over her shaves glistening skin. She sits on the arm of his chair, draping her leg over Orleans, now using his moistened fingers as tools for her pleasure.

LA is lying back as his servers dress rises up around her waist. She spreads her legs and dips down over him as he opens his mouth Michael sees the tips of his tongue protruding and prodding as she lowers herself to meet his hungry lips.

Michael is helpless, blood surging, a throbbing growing fighting against the material in his pants to be free. Without free will or bodily control, he watches as his pants zipper is loosed and she takes him in her hand. Licking her lips she looks up at him, he is frozen. She places her hands cupping him as she is about to take him into her mouth.

71.

The sun is barely visible in the sky as the men are awake from an unnaturally deep sleep. Michael is feeling disoriented, almost borderline nausea. They are to gather in the dining hall by seven sharp. He steps into the waterfall shower, making an attempt at washing away the cobwebs still stubbornly populating his head.

The water feels warm, refreshing. He remembers vague glimpses of the previous evening, but he is uncertain if they are remnants of a dream of if they are fragments of reality. He clearly remembers Elemental making the toast to our future. He can remember moving into the library. The cigars, from there the images become wet paint that someone has brushed out in every direction. Splashes of color, moments of sound, heat the cold. The more he attempts at recalling, the harder it seems to do so. He shakes his head, he is feeling better and he needs to get suited up for the day's activities.

He turns off the water, wraps the thick, soft white cotton towel around his waist and heads to sink to shave. Looking in the mirror he thinks Damn, I look like hell.

New Orleans Man sits on the edge of his bed, rubbing his neck, "God help me, I hope I didn't catch some weird jungle juice fever or sumptin." He tries to stand but needs to gold onto the dresser to steady himself. He retraces the previous even and remembers something about butterflies and souls. "I'm from da home and heart of Hoodoo and Voodoo and der's sum seriously weird shit going on down heya."

*

New York is lying in bed. The room is spinning like the days when he would drink apple moonshine with his buddies up on the roof of his old building. Putting his floor on the floor next to him, attempting to stop the spinning he starts dry heaving.

"Holy shit. I didn't even get the name of the fuckin truck that ran me over."

*

L.A. made it to the shower letting the water run over him. He is suffering from the worst case of cotton mouth. Gargling with the shower water is not solving it. He remembers the servers clearing the table, than Elemental appeared. Everyone toasted to something or another. Cigars. Then he woke up here. What kinda trouble could he have gotten into on an island designed to help him? Now, if he could get the construction crew behind his left eye to stop hammering he would be fine.

72.

The culinary staff is preparing a hearty breakfast of eggs, sausage, toast, hash browns, fruit, pancakes, waffles coffee and juice. The one staff member adds a nameless powder to all beverages, including the sparkling water and the eggs. The servers from last night are all in attendance, dressed in crisp white linen sous chef attire, their nails are short, painted nude. Hair is covered with black chef beanies. They are purely androgynous.

The men start to wander in, looking worse for the wear. . The staff seats them, without a flicker of recognition from either side.

73.

Elemental is in his office watching the security cameras, rubbing his hands together with anticipation as if he were a child awaiting a birthday party. "It's finally here. Everything is going according to plan!"

Near him, a man dressed in black speaks in hushed tones. He is almost straining to be heard.

"I got in late last night. I thought I could catch you before the day's..." He clears his throat. "...activities start?"

"What a pleasant surprise. I thought for sure you wouldn't be able to pull away from work and your other responsibilities. I am so happy you could join us" Elemental walks over to him, placing his hand on the broad black suited gentlemen's back. The man is dressed in black jeans, a tight black t-shirt and black boots. He moves away from the glow of the CC TV's and stands in the shadows.

"I decided it was in both of our best interest if I could be here for the inaugural execution of our plan. After all of our hard work, I wouldn't miss this for the world." He turns and lights a cigarette, "I am on a damage control mission for work. I had to take the red eye from Rome last night. Thank God, I share my responsibilities with a very good friend who was most accommodating."

"Ah, what are friends for? Shall you join us for breakfast?"

"Thank you, but I am a bit tired after the trip. I've eaten breakfast already. I believe that I will take a shower and try to catch a few minutes of rest before things—kick off?"

"Very well, you always have known best."

The man in black responded with a throaty laugh as he exhaled his final drag of his cigarette.

"I shall see you at eight a.m. The activities shall start at eight sharp, and I don't want you to miss anything."

"I wouldn't miss it for the world."

74.

The men are finishing breakfast. Elemental is walking to the head of the table. He approaches each man, exchanging pleasantries like an owner of a small restaurant. As he reaches his place he looks across at the faces of the guests gathered here, together ""I trust you all slept well last night?"

Michael looks toward the other men, and answers under his breath "Oddly enough, I never slept like that in my life. Must be the air here. I didn't wake up, or even dream. I don't remember much after dinner." The three men nod and grunt in agreement.

"Wonderful. Shall we go to the Great Room? We have a few things to go over." Elemental lifts his glass and all of the men drink to the events that await them.

Within the few minutes between breakfast and the time it takes to gather in the great room the energy starts to shift. There is a palpable buzz. Something is happening. The men are starting to snap at one another. A fist fight almost breaks out. The staff is double today. Each man has two handlers.

Elemental claps his hands sharply to get the groups attention. "We have imported some very exotic animals for today's safari which I am sure you will favor. For those of you who shoot and kill, we have a famous taxidermist here from the Washington DC National Nature Museum so you can enjoy your trophies later." Elemental was pleased with himself, "Gentlemen, please follow your guest service representative. They will brief you on your mission and the equipment."

The men all split off from one another.

75.

The prisoners are a bit sluggish today despite their chance at freedom. They're excited yet distrustful. The energy is palpable. Dawn is just about to break, the humidity is at 80% and the heat is almost unbearable this early in the day.

Armed handlers are bountiful, and each prisoner is assigned a specific handler. The men hired are African militant types with a bloodlust and lack of conscience.

The Major handler appears in front of the group to make an announcement, "You will be receiving your directions. If you try or plan to do anything that you have not been directed to do, please know you will be shot. It was my personal pleasure having each of you and it will be my personal pleasure to be the one to pull the trigger."

The prisoner from LA mumbles inaudibly and is hit with the butt of a machine gun. He responds in a heavy Spanish accent 'Sir, yes sir."

Kione is standing beside him, he nods his head, averts his eyes and laughs like a child at a circus. His handler pistol-whips him and he is so numb from violence and pain it doesn't affect him in the least.

The Major walks over to Kione "I didn't just hear that outta your mouth?

He pistol-whips Kione again, this time with ferocity.

76.

The men are completely dressed in army fatigues and armed with Barrett REC7 military assault rifles. They are being briefed on their missions, each handed a confidential manila envelope.

Elemental inspects them, pleased with the progress they have made. "I hope you are all as excited as I am about today's mission. You all have a satellite phone on your person at all times. Once you have completed your mission, please call back to home base and we will retrieve you at once. If at any time you feel you are in imminent danger, we will have staff on the course that will always be within a few minutes of you to ensure your safety."

*

The line of prisoners is motionless. Kione, New York, LA, New Orleans and the rest of the men all stand silently waiting their release.

*

"That being said, please keep in mind we are not dealing with humans, so you cannot allow yourself to be lulled into a false sense of security. These are wild animals -- if they have a chance, they will kill you." Elemental continued with his briefing.

The men start to get antsy with anticipation. Even the men who are usually ardently against hunting are salivating at the chance to kill.

"Please open you information packets. You will find all of the information you will need on your chosen prey."

The men open their packets and are confused and suspicious. Michael discovers his prey is Kione. L.A. Man's prey is the man who cut his daughters tongue out. Each man realizes that the prey they are hunting is the man who ruined his family.

"Gentlemen, I believe you will be very pleased with the work and the many hours that went into picking your exact prey."

Michael is shaking his head, fighting against the excitement and rage intensifying inside of him. "Whoa... this is some kind of an exercise, right? You don't actually expect us to hunt down..."

L.A. looks over his information, "M-my prayers have been answered! It is an honor to rid the world of..."

New York snaps in retort. "All the hours I spent studying this son of a bitch, watching him torment..."

"I'd kill him! Any of you who can't -- I'll kill the animals who hurt you too. It'd be an honor, do my family proud!" New Orleans testified.

"Men, do you feel that you can't perform the mission that is put before you? Is there anyone who feels that they cannot go onto the next level?" Elemental poses the question with such resolve none of the men would think to do anything but what is being presented to them.

The men answer in perfect unison, "No. No sir, no."

"I am ready. Come on you son of a bitch, let's roll." Michael psyches himself as if Kione can actually hear what he is saying.

The flashbacks are coming, and they are fast and they are crystal clear, as if they are looking at a news bite- Jilly is being beaten then left alone with Joe's dead body.

*

Orleans man's wife and daughter, the wife begging for her daughter's freedom, bargaining with all she has to offer, her body and her life.

*

L.A's daughter, one man holding her mouth open while a machete is being swung, gagging screams with a spray of blood that seems to cover everything in the room.

*

New York's daughter is looking directly into the webcam begging for her daddy to make the monster stop, crying asking what she did to make him so mean to her.

77.

The men move to the waiting jeeps, walking with military precision. Each man climbs into his designated ride with an armed driver and a guide. At the same time the prisoners are being blindfolded, and put in the back of military personnel jeep with guns pointed at them, and jabbing their ribs and backs during the entire ride. Each man and prisoner is dropped off at the assigned destinations.

Elemental is watching all of the action from his private office. Every screen has a close up of the hunter and the prey.

Michael jumps with his guide out of the jeep. "Eye for an eye Mother Fucker."

The guide checks Michael's gun fires a warning shot and makes sure the gun is in perfect working order. Hands the gun to Michael with a slap on the arm and nods as he disappears back into the early dawn shadows.

The expedition commences, warning shots ring throughout the jungle.

"How the fuck did I get into this? Am I really here?" Michael hears a motor off in the distance. As his senses adjust to the jungle sounds and the light becomes stronger, through the filter of the jungle, he realizes that he hears movement a few yards away.

Kione is pushed out of the jeep and beat one last time with the muzzle of the gun, right before his blindfold is removed. He inhales sharply. He is disoriented but knows instinctually to go away from the sound of the jeep.

Michael squats down, allowing instinct to drive him. He no longer can think or fell, his emotions are totally mute. His body and mind are voracious in their appetite to kill. He has one picture in his head. He no longer has sweet memories Merl, the joy and laughter of Jilly and Joe, the only thing he can see if the face of his prey. The only thing he can hear is the sound of that voice. Michael has turned into a predator in this jungle. He senses seem to be mutating, magnifying with every minute that passes. Now, thoughts of his children, pictures of the crime scenes are rushing him. Hundreds per second, vengeance running through his veins like blood.

Kione starts to walk gingerly becoming familiar with the jingle landscape at his feet. He is weak and sore and physically stretched to the limit but the adrenaline pumping mixed with the thought of freedom has given him a renewed sense of urgency.

Michael waits, hearing the footsteps getting close. Sweat runs down his face, heart pounds, he can hear his blood pumping through the arteries.

A few miles west L.A. is feeling at ease familiar with the weapon at his side from the years he spent in San Diego and in Iraq and

Afghanistan, fighting the war. He flashes back to the days as a soldier then back to the present moment. All of his senses are peaked. His training from the Marines is kicking back in. He is poised, ready to kill at a moment's notice. Like a cheetah he is stealth, he is poised and he is unstoppable once he has his prey in his sight.

New Orleans is a bit shaky sitting propped against a tree. Elemental sees this and is concerned, "Orleans, do not answer me aloud. Can you read me? Are you alright?"

He responds with a nod. He looks at his hands clasping the weapon and his mind is taking back to the hot day when they made him go to the M.E and identify the bodies. They hadn't even cleaned them up yet. There they were, once the essence of this and love now waxy mummifications only resembling who and what they once were. Waves of hate washed over him.

Looking over the jungle he realized this is his chance to make it right. This is his chance to stop this cock sucker from ever doing this to anyone else. He looks up to the sky and makes the sign of the cross as he hears a distinctly human movement about 100 yards away. He cocks his weapon and lies down on his stomach in sniper position.

New York is uncomfortable. He is more reserved and more effeminate and scholarly then the others. His pulse is racing. His clothes are soaked through with sweat and he is shaking. He straightens his back, sets his jaw. As he looked at his weapon he felt stronger, crueler and more focused than he ever had before. "I will do this. I will do this for every child that has been in the news, for every day I watched my daughter, every tear me and my family shed. I will do this for every father who ever lost his child." He becomes visibly calmer and kisses the gun as if it was the hand of a lover.

His prisoner is coming upon him.

Footsteps on jungle carpet, the crunch of the rotting brush underneath unsuspecting feet. Each convict fleeing, frenzied, mad with hunger, psychologically fragile or broken from the days of torture they had to endure. Some of them lame a leg or an arm from infection, venom or fractures caused by the punishing beatings of hooded guards under the cloak of night. After being kept in the dark for so many days on end, their eyes burned and teared when subjected to the sunlight.

78.

Back at the lodge Elemental is finally starting to relax. Now, the only thing he is worried about is time. He lights up a cigar and pours himself a Glen Fiddich 50 YO, neat and offers one to his guest.

Nodding and lighting his own Cuban he makes an observation, "The amazing thing about criminal minds is that they can rationalize their actions and move on with their lives as if nothing they did was any fault of their own. They can blame their upbringing, their parents, the school, the bullies, the gang members, that uncle who molested them or the mother who never loved them.

These men and women are predators in every sense of the word. Many of them are sociopaths. Superficial yet charming, they possess above average intelligence. They can fool even the brightest among us with their sincere insincerity. Have you ever known one to show the least amount of remorse or an iota of shame over their vile crimes against humanity?"

Elemental takes a long sip, letting the whisky coat his tongue swirling it around his mouth before he swallows, allowing him to savor this moment. "For all intents and purposes these so called people are egocentric narcissists. They have never felt love nor have they ever considered what it is to attach to anything on an emotional level. I did notice that they are generally unresponsiveness to any interpersonal relations, romantic or platonic. Sex is purely mechanical, enjoyed only for the dopamine I suppose. The predilection for prostitutes and sexual deviance is only one of the manifestations."

Both men turn to the wall of screens, zooming in and out on each man. They keep one camera on Michael and Kione at all times seeming to have a pointed interest in the outcome of this hunt.

The men are vibrating with anticipation, eyes to the scope of the guns. The sun is gaining strength with every passing tic of the clock. Steam rising from the jungle floor, the birds, and insects, the wind rustling the upper canopy- any movements are amplified making the sounds feel as if they are being generated inside their heads, plucking their nerves like electroshock. The sound of their pulse, the whoosh of blood pumping through their veins blending with the cacophony of sounds taking every ounce of restraint to stay focused on the task at hand.

Fingers cocking triggers with the tough of a feather, weapons poised and nestled into the crook of their necks. The men have found the sweet spot, each primed to take down the demon that has made its home in his life, in his head since that day.

79.

A film reel is running now, straddled between memories and reality, the men are fighting it to stay in the here and now. Oblivious to everything now- the rollercoaster has begun.

The New York Prisoner is slowly, methodically finding the safest way though the untamed jungle. He stops every few yards to gauge his next move. He will be damned if a trip on a vine or a broken bone will stop him now. Soon enough he will be in Denmark or the Thailand doing what he does best in a warm and welcoming atmosphere.

New York is with his family enjoying a movie on the beach for their family outing to Coney Island, snap turn, his tortured baby girl, loop turn, in the jungle, click, click, click, "daddy help me" up, up, up, The S.W.A.T. team pounds at his door, New York is waiting in the background to hold his girl again, he inhales deeply and takes aim, spiraling down now at breakneck speed, drop, he is out of his seat his stomach drops with the ground out from under him, shots fired.

Strutting, stopping to urinate against a tree the prisoner from New Orleans is day dreaming about starting over, maybe somewhere in the northwest, mighty big county out der. Nuh body would know 'em or know of 'em.

New Orleans is on a ride of his own, but he is walking through a fun house, everything is slow motion. He enters to a moving family scene of his family going to church and walking the Garden District, he sees the bastard pop out from behind the corner, he turns where he is with his girls, decorating their costumes for Mardi Gras, the demon appears, laughing, taunting he runs after him into morose tableau of his dead family when they were found. He is sick he looks up and again sees the monsters face somewhere in the distance he hears shots ring out. He turns to look again, this time there is his pray, laying on his side, blood pouring from his mouth and ears, begging him for help.

L.A. prisoner squares his shoulders, spitting, focusing, planning as he takes the jungle like it is his to own. He has that cocky gangbanger strut. He may visit the Cartel while he is away, make this a business trip.

L.A. is in war mode. He is back in the mountains of Afghanistan. A hungry marine tracking a Taliban member when he turns a corner and enters a cave he is with his daughter at her communion. She is dressed in white and he is so in love he can't see anyone or anything else, she reaches over to him and whispers, he hears footsteps, he is on the chase. The cave winds deeper into the mountain, he hears men laughing as he turns he sees his girl walking away from the house with her dog and best friend, whispering and laughing the way young girls do. The scene fades and transforms into his daughter scared to leave the house writing on a pad, pleading, tears in her eyes, don't make me go. Now he is waiting still of motion, not breathing, sweating and shaking as if any second he is about to explode. He stands, inhales sharply filling his lungs with the oxygenated sweet air. He is back now in reality, looking down he opens his fly and pisses on the dying man at his feet.

Kione walks very gingerly. He is very distrustful by nature he turns a 360 looking up at the trees, down at the boulders and the brush. "Dad, I know you're here somewhere. I love you, Daddy." He kneels down lifting a fern.

"Do you really believe that?" Now he is starting to laugh his maniacal, dark, sadistic laugh. "I hate you, you rotten son of a bitch. I was your experiment gone wrong. I was your fucking lab rat. You perverted mother fucker. You expected me to break, you expected me to melt so you could rebuild me."

He picks up a huge rock and throws it toward a branch with a micro lens knocking it out of focus. "Was there anything you could throw at me that could break me? You couldn't win then, you sure as hell won't win now. You hate me because I'm smarter then you. You hate me because I am better-looking than you. You couldn't handle that I am a better version of you and you wanted me gone."

He tramples the vines and picks up the wireless microphone, yelling into it. "Want some of me? Bring it on! Come on dear Father of mine, I'm waiting. You don't have the balls. You like adversaries that can't fight back. You prey on the weak. You never had any balls, did you? I have enough for both of us. Darwin mother fucker. Only the strong survive. J.E., if you had only used me as a protégé, we could have done amazing things together. I know you have your dirty little paws in this you fuckin animal. You made it out of the slums, but the slums never made it out of you. Careful what you wish for, old man, you just might get it. I'll hunt your sorry..."

Michael sees Kione, hears him but he starts to fade away. He is sitting back at his home, in his favorite chair watching family videos of their wedding, then the couple on Christmas morning with the kids and Dozer. He is comfortable, he is happy as the next movie plays of he and his wife making love in Yosemite when the kids disappeared. His mouth is dry, he feels like he is burning from the inside out. Back in the jungle, Michael, clenches jaw, leaning against the tree, turns his head sharply and vomits.

The men now process that this is that pivotal moment when the hunter becomes the prey and the realization that their life is over as they once knew it. They can never go back, it will never be the same and neither will they.

80.

The sun is setting, over the mountainous backdrop casting a red and gold glow through the epic windows. The men are back from their excursions. They are showered and dressed for the final evening ceremony, drinking brandy, not sure is the events of the day were reality or just another psychotropic trip they have taken. Yes, they are each very aware that part of the emersion therapy has been drug induced hallucinations meant to erase all of their individual inhibitions and allow the true root of their grief and hate and heartache bubble to the surface.

They are immersed in conversations but nothing is mentioned about the experience they shared earlier today. That has been the common denominator this entire trip, nothing is ever mentioned about the out of the ordinary, about the morose or the perverse or the sadistic or the vile.

Elemental greets the group, each man looking a bit haggard, a bit worse for the ware. "Gentlemen, welcome back. I want to congratulate you, you each are exceptional marksmen. Please join me in the trophy room."

This is the first hint that today's trip might have actually been a reality. The men all follow their host and the staff to the trophy room, apprehensive to what they will find.

The sun has set, the darkness is dripping over the lodge, oozing in through the corners. The heat of the day escaping leaving a chill in the air, the room is cavernous and dimly lit.

Elemental holds forth. "Friends -- your transition is now complete. You have made the metamorphosis from victim to victor, cheers! You have done society and the world a service that can never be repaid. You, men, are the fundamental building blocks of a new order. I would like to present you with your trophies!"

Panels go down in the walls to expose inset curio cabinets made of glass- lit from inside, as spotlights focus on the trophy it holds.

The men look behind them to find a ghastly menagerie of "trophies". To their complete horror is the man who murdered their families, stuffed and placed in a submissive position with fear and horror on their face for eternity. A human exhibition of some of the world's most evil remains. They pass glancing at one another's "trophies" until they stop in front of their kill.

Elemental could not be more pleased, "Gentlemen, if you will excuse me, I am going to get washed up for dinner. Please, make yourselves comfortable and celebrate, for this is a historic day!"

The men are silent, retracing the past week, separating fact from fiction. Trying to pinpoint the exact moment they transformed from victim to become judge, jury and executioner. The room was so still, so silent one could hear a pin drop, their shallow breath barely audible. Shock, penance, relief, fear, desperation churning into a wave of emotions that lapped at their feet then rolled back out replaced with relief, pride and savory revenge.

81

Elemental is back in his office, watching the reaction of the men. Quite positive that he has single handedly changed the scales of justice worldwide. He has made the largest sociological, psychological and ethical breakthrough in the history of mankind.

"This worked out perfectly, and I could never have done it without you! You made your uncle very proud, Eric. I think we made wonderful business partners. You are the son I always wanted, my sister was right about you from the moment I held you in my arms in Loma Linda. She said you were born under an enchanted star. That day I felt like I was holding my own."

Eric was dressed in black as usual sitting with his signature black boots propped atop the desk. He thinks back to the meetings with the wardens, the prisoner transfers. All that time having his firm back in California. He's not completely sure he would have done it if the stars hadn't aligned, if it wasn't for the Mitchell brothers, and wasn't for his only cousin Kione murdering and raping his son Joey.

"Thanks. I owe everything I am to you Uncle J. You know we named Joey after you, Joseph Norwood Mitchell. I believe Merl told Michael Norwood was an old family name." Eric laughed stoically, "Partners, yeah, we certainly do make a good pair."

Eric picks up a picture of Elemental aka J.E. holding his son, Kione as a child. Kione is blowing out birthday candles on a cake with his name in icing in an "I Love You Dad" frame.

He sets it atop the newspaper of Kione's arrest.

"You know, my mom never was a very good photographer. I remember that party like it was yesterday. I was always so jealous of Kione when we were kids. Cousins have a weird relationship anyway I guess. I always thought he had it all, looks, charm, you as a dad. Everything a kid could ever want. Than my mom got sick and I went away…" Eric let his thoughts trail off.

J.E. walked over to Eric and gave him a long, overdo hug.

"I love you more than if you were my son, as long as I am here you will always have family."